THE DOLL'S HAND

Richard Sherwick

SOFTWOOD BOOKS

SUFFOLK, UK

Published and Manufactured by Softwood Books

EU Responsible person: Maddy Glenn
Office 2, Wharfside House, Prentice Road, Stowmarket, Suffolk, IP14 1RD
www.softwoodbooks.com
hello@softwoodbooks.com

EU Rep:
Authorised Rep Compliance Ltd., Ground Floor, 71 Lower Baggot Street,
Dublin, D02 P593, Ireland
www.arccompliance.com
info@arccompliance.com

Paperback ISBN: 978-1-0684103-0-7

Contents

Chapter 1

Should she, or shouldn't she?

Gilly, aged twelve, had found the hand of a china doll in an antique chest stored in some outbuildings in her parents' garden. She opened the drawers, hoping to find the rest of the doll, or at least some other parts, but she found nothing.

How strange, she thought.

Gilly was about to put the hand in her pocket, but an uneasy feeling made her hesitate. Perhaps the hand should remain in the drawer, and maybe she should forget about it. Perhaps if she asked her parents first? But they wouldn't care. She could always have anything she wanted.

Still, Gilly hesitated as to whether to take the hand or not. A jumble of thoughts went through her mind. *Who owned the doll? How had it come to be broken? Was it given as a birthday or Christmas present? The young owner must have been heartbroken when it was damaged.* She thought for a moment, realising this would make a good story. She could write it, and then, when she returned

1

to school after her summer holidays, it would give her something to read to the class rather than describing the family holiday. The Raymonds usually went away for a long summer break, very often overseas. However, this year was different. Her father, Charles, was a solicitor and owned a law firm in Aldbridge, the nearby town. The firm was very busy, and Charles was unable to take a break. Instead, they would have Christmas in Austria or Switzerland. Her father was a keen skier and Gilly was looking forward to trying herself. Her mother, Julia, was a florist who had a small shop, also in the nearby town. She had plans to relocate to the outbuildings in their garden.

Gilly once again picked up the hand. She could borrow it, write her story, and return it unharmed in a few days. She felt happier. She put the hand in her pocket, and closed the drawer. Gilly returned to their large old farmhouse – far too large for her and her parents, but her father was very successful and enjoyed the largest and the best of everything.

Julia was in the kitchen looking through the post. Gilly reached into her pocket and removed the china hand.

"Mummy, I found this hand in a chest in the barn. Isn't it fascinating?"

Julia looked over her glasses.

"Well, if you say so, darling." She didn't share her daughter's excitement. "What will you do with it?"

"I'll write a story about it and read it in class when I go

back to school in September."

Julia frowned. "You will still help me out in the florists, won't you? It'll be getting busy soon."

"Definitely!" Gilly replied, excited. She loved helping out at the shop.

Gilly went to her room, reached into her pocket, and pulled out the doll's hand. Even now she had reservations. Should she leave it here or return it to the barn? She opened her desk drawer and carefully placed it beside her other treasures.

That afternoon, she played in the garden with her lovely brown-and-white spaniel, Lola. Gilly adored her. On long summer days, Gilly and her mother would often visit one of the nearby beaches. They both loved swimming, as did Lola.

Gilly had few friends, but those few were special. Her closest was a boy called Jimmy Shaw, the son of a property developer, and often Julia would collect him on the way to the seaside. Gilly's father worked long days, so she was usually alone with her mother well into the evening.

That evening, when it was Gilly's bedtime (not that there was a regular time, or that her mother would make her go to bed – she usually decided for herself), Gilly bathed and put on her pyjamas. Lola was lying on the landing outside her room. Gilly climbed into bed, knowing that Lola would follow. Lola was supposed to sleep in her dog bed on

Gilly's bedroom floor, but in the mornings she was always lying in Gilly's bed beside her. Gilly kept calling, "Lola! Lola!", but all Lola would do was tilt her head one way then the other, staying on the landing. Gilly felt drowsy, and soon tired of Lola's response. When she woke the following morning, there was no Lola beside her. She shook her head.

"Strange girl," she said.

With that, she climbed out of bed and dressed for breakfast. In the kitchen, Gilly found her mother making some toast, her father sitting at the table reading his newspaper, and Lola lying in her basket.

"Well, what happened to you?" Gilly asked. She knelt down beside Lola and made a fuss of her.

"Wasn't she with you overnight?" her mother asked.

"No," replied Gilly. "She's behaving rather strangely."

"It has been very warm during the evenings. I expect it's much cooler in here," her mother replied.

Gilly sat down at the table opposite her father.

"Good morning, Daddy."

Her father gave a grunt. Julia placed a plate of toast on the table and Gilly tucked in. After a few minutes, her father folded his paper and looked at his watch.

"Daddy," said Gilly.

"Yes," replied her father in his deep tone.

"There is a small chest in the barn. I opened the drawers and found the hand of a china doll in the second drawer.

May I keep it?" she asked.

Her father replied, "You can have the chest and anything else you find in the barn."

"No, just the hand, that's all." Gilly said.

"Well, can I buy you a complete doll? You don't have to play with broken pieces."

"There's something about the hand," Gilly explained. "Something strange and intriguing."

Her father shrugged. "I'll be late," he said, as he stood up and walked towards the door.

"We'll see you tomorrow then," said Julia.

"Goodbye, Daddy!" Gilly called after him.

"Yes," Charles replied in a gruff voice.

It wasn't unusual for Charles to spend long hours at the office. Gilly couldn't help thinking what a busy man her father was. However, Julia knew that he had other interests, especially with the young ladies in the practice. She didn't really care. He earned a lot of money, and both Julia and Gilly could buy anything they wished for – although she kept this from her daughter. There were plenty of things about their lives that Gilly didn't need to know.

Chapter 2

The long summer days continued, with Gilly enjoying her visits to the beach, and helping her mother in the florists. Life was good, and Gilly wished the summer would last forever. Eventually there was an overcast day, mild and warm but with some drizzle.

Right, thought Gilly. *Today would be ideal to make a start on my story about the china doll's hand.* After breakfast, she sat in her bedroom at her desk, opened her notepad, and picked up her pen. On her desk, she also laid the doll's hand.

Gilly started to write.

There was a family. Their name was Conway – Mike and Daphne Conway, with a daughter named Emma. They lived in Westbrook, a village in Suffolk. Their house was quite modern and spacious. Both Mike and Daphne worked, and they had a comfortable lifestyle. They loved and spoiled Emma. She had everything she wanted, and even had two bedrooms to herself! One Christmas she was given many presents, which she would cherish. One present she liked above all the rest was a medium-sized china doll. The doll was fabulous, she thought, and named her 'Bedina'.

A year or two passed, but she never tired of her lovely doll. Emma always treated her with love, care and respect. The doll's height was around twelve to fourteen inches. She had long brown curly hair, and her face was very realistic, which looked attractive rather than sickly and pretty. The dress she wore was made from quality material, maroon in colour with a cream cardigan. Her shoes were brown leather, and could be removed. All of her joints moved and could be put into any position.

Gilly paused. *Emma had a life similar to hers,* she thought. *What a lucky girl she was.*

Daphne had a brother who lived in Carlisle in the North of England. His name was John Ross Newton. His wife was Margaret, and they had a son called Simon who was the same age as his cousin, Emma. They all tried to meet once a year, either on holidays or short visits. Emma didn't care for Simon. He was very clever with a natural talent for drawing.

One evening during the winter months, John and Margaret Newton were driving on a remote road. The weather conditions became awful. It was freezing and also began to snow. On a sharp bend, John lost control. Their car skidded and left the road, dropping down a steep hillside.

The car rolled and rolled until it reached the bottom. John and Margaret were barely alive. There they would stay for many hours until their injuries and the cold took their lives.

Simon, who had been staying with neighbours while his parents were away, was now an orphan and in need of a secure home. After the funeral, Mike and Daphne were approached about Simon. He had become very distressed after the loss of his parents. He liked his aunt and uncle, and being with them at the funeral make him feel better and not alone. This was clear to the neighbour, so she suggested that Mike and Daphne should consider giving him a good home. Mike and Daphne had thought about this, and the only reason they weren't certain was because of Emma. Eventually they would agree to raise Simon. Now came the awkward part – to tell Emma.

Emma could not believe this. She would have to share her home with Simon, her cousin who she didn't really like. On enquiring where he would sleep, she was told Simon would have the spare room. Emma didn't recognise a spare room. It was her second room. She stormed off, ran upstairs and into her main bedroom, slamming the door behind her. She was full of rage, picked up the nearest thing – her favourite doll – and without even thinking, pulled the hand from the arm.

She sat down on the bed. What had she done? Still

*in a fit of rage, she threw her doll into the corner of the
room.*

Gilly stopped writing. Where was all this coming from?
It was as if the story was writing itself. At school, she had
always written stories – good stories with excellent marks
– but she always had to think hard about what she would
write, and then introduce some changes. Writing this story
was very different. The ideas were already there.

She stopped for a while, and her mother called her
downstairs for lunch.

"Shall we go out this afternoon?" her mother asked as
they sat at the table.

Gilly thought for a moment. "No, thank you. I want to
keep writing my story."

"Is it going well?" her mother asked.

"Very well," replied Gilly.

After they had eaten, Gilly returned to her room and
picked up her pen once again. The ideas flowed into her
mind.

*Simon did go to live with Mike and Daphne. It wasn't easy at
first, especially with Emma, who was quite horrible to him.
Things did improve when one day Simon drew a portrait of
Emma. She was an attractive girl, and his attention to detail
showed her real beauty. Emma hadn't realised before how*

gifted he was. After this she was much kinder to him. Still not ideal, but much more respectful, especially because he had lost both of his parents. The four of them did become united as a family, and Simon's childhood was as happy as it could be. Things would change a few years later.

Although Daphne and Mike were working, Mike enjoyed gambling, usually playing cards. He started to lose serious money and soon things spiralled out of control. He was forced to tell Daphne they were in serious debt. She couldn't believe what she was hearing. They argued, discussed, argued again, and things really hit rock bottom when their house was repossessed. They really had nothing else to give and nowhere to go.

Again, Gilly wondered where all this was coming from. Emma's life didn't sound like her life any more, and she wondered what would happen to the family. Intrigued, she kept writing.

Daphne worked for the bishop as his secretary, a job she had done for many years. She had to tell him about their situation, and he was saddened to hear about it. He sat back in his chair and revealed there was an empty house owned by the church. The house was large and remote. However, it was in good order and he felt it would make a very good home for them all. Daphne had a great feeling of relief, and told the bishop she could not thank him enough. It wasn't long before the Conways moved into Underwood House. Daphne had taken to looking after all the finances so Mike could never again lose even a penny.

Emma didn't like the location of Underwood House. It was too much off the beaten track and too old fashioned, and she knew that, because it didn't belong to her parents, nothing was really going to change. They did make it their home, and decorated it tastefully, so they were mostly happy. Daphne arranged to take on some additional work so there was never any rent to pay, and gradually they got back on their feet.

Emma left school and worked in a nearby town. She worked in some office doing menial tasks, but she was keen to progress. Simon was very different. He chose to stay at school and hoped to go to university. Money had been, and still was, tight. There were never any holidays, and their cars were several years old. It would help if Simon was working, but they knew he was too clever, and one day he would reward them.

One evening, Daphne revealed their financial situation would soon change. She wouldn't say how, but she was very optimistic. Mike knew his wife was serious, and said he would give her his full support.

Gilly decided she needed a rest. Perhaps she could help her

mother, or ask for more visits to the beach, as the holidays were coming to an end.

On several occasions, Gilly returned to her story. However, unlike before when the ideas had come instantly, she could think of nothing else to write. She closed her eyes and thought hard, but all she saw were shadows in black and dark grey. This annoyed her, as she was looking forward to reading her story in class when she returned to school. Gilly mentioned this to her mother.

"Well, darling. This is what's known as writer's block, I believe. You'll soon have some more ideas," her mother said, reassuringly.

Gilly tried several more times to write, but there were no more ideas. Instead, she enjoyed the rest of her holiday and concentrated on her school work.

Before school resumed, Julia asked her daughter to tidy her room, which had become messy over the holidays. Gilly was given a box to put the things in she would like to keep. Anything else not tidied away would go in the dustbin.

Gilly started with her desk. There were several stones and shells she had found on the beach, interesting pieces of wood, photos she had taken, postcards from classmates, dried flower arrangements she had made. All of these went into the box to be kept.

And what of the doll's hand and her story? Well, they might as well go in. They would go up into the attic and, if she wanted, they could be returned. Gilly tied the box with some coloured string and gave it to her mother. Later that afternoon, Julia climbed into the attic and stored the box safely for another time.

That evening, when Gilly climbed into bed, she noticed Lola had joined her, and was lying in her dog bed.

"What a strange girl you are," said Gilly. "All summer you've deserted me, and now you've decided to return. Welcome back, then."

Chapter 3

December 1993
Eighteen Years Later

Much to her father's surprise, Gilly had rejected a career in law, and joining him in the practice. Instead, she chose to become a teacher, and taught at the local primary school at Finches Green. She enjoyed her work, and was very well-liked. Her father had had a horrific skiing accident some years earlier, and was paralysed from the waist down. He now lived in Hardingfield, an exclusive nursing home where he could still carry out some work. However, he had become very moody. Gilly's mother still lived in the farmhouse and continued a small amount of floristry work from there.

Gilly and her mother were often mistaken for sisters. Both were tall, and toned from years of swimming, skiing and outdoor pursuits. Gilly's shoulder-length light-brown hair suited her kind, rounded face. While Julia was slightly taller, with a heart-shaped face, tanned skin, and longer, straight brown hair, it was obvious that they were related. Gilly took after Julia, and her mother still looked youthful.

Gilly had moved to a large apartment on the ground floor of a converted country house in Charnham. Her friend Jimmy Shaw's company had carried out the conversion, and she had been able to select exactly what she wanted. Gilly was still single, which suited her. There had been male friends, but no one was ever serious, and she really enjoyed her freedom. She was close to her mother and close to Jimmy, but only as a friend. On Tuesday evenings Gilly and some of the other teachers from local schools would meet at a pub or restaurant for a social evening. They enjoyed trying out different places, but they had some favourites where they had become regular visitors.

On this Tuesday, Gilly and her colleagues met up at the Fleur-de-Lys at Jays Common. They enjoyed coming here for the roaring fires, along with the good ales and food. The pub was brick and flint with a rather worn thatched roof, and inside there were several secluded nooks and crannies with tables and seating. It was early December and rather cold, so the group chose a table beside the open fire.

During the evening, Gilly needed to visit the toilets, which were situated towards the end of the room and in view of their table. On her return, she noticed a rather attractive young man sitting at a table towards the front window, out of view from her friends. He was blonde-haired, blue-eyed, and dressed in smart-casual clothes. He noticed Gilly looking towards him and gave her a friendly smile.

The man was all alone. He had no drink or food, and was surrounded by empty tables.

Gilly felt a strange hesitation. *Should she, or shouldn't she?*

She glanced back at her friends, who were deep in conversation. When she looked back, the man smiled again. Intrigued, she walked over to where he was sitting.

"Hello," said Gilly.

"Good evening," replied the man.

"I haven't seen you here before."

"Oh, I haven't visited the area for some while," he replied.

Gilly sat down and introduced herself.

"Very pleased to meet you," said the man, who introduced himself as Simon Newton.

Simon was well-spoken and very polite. They chatted for some time, and Gilly discovered Simon was an architect, and at some time in the past he had lived locally.

Gilly asked Simon to join her friends for the rest of the evening. Simon declined, saying he really must be on his way.

"Well, I hope to see you again soon, Simon," Gilly told him.

Simon replied with a smile. "Of that, I am sure," he said.

Gilly stood up and held her hand out for Simon to take.

However, he made no attempt to stand or touch her. Instead, he thanked her for her company and said, "Good evening, Gilly."

Now Gilly was standing up, she was just in view of her friends' table. A couple of them saw her and called her over.

"Goodbye, Simon," she said.

He smiled once again as she left. Gilly wondered why he hadn't just shaken her hand or asked for her details – she had really enjoyed their conversation. On returning to her friends, they asked where she had been. She told them about the good-looking Simon, and her friends insisted that Simon should join them.

Allan, another teacher from Gilly's school, stood up to look for him. He walked around the corner to the front window where Gilly had been, and soon returned saying there was no one there.

"He must be there," replied Gilly. "I would have noticed if he'd left."

Allan went to check the toilets, and could find no trace of Simon. The conversation changed and the evening continued as usual, although Simon was still on Gilly's mind, and his words when she hoped to see him again.

She wondered about his reply, *Of that I'm sure.*

When the group left the pub, Gilly spoke to the landlord, asking him if he had seen a man who matched Simon's description. He had never seen anyone like him, on that evening or at any other time, to his knowledge. Gilly took a final look at where he had been sitting. There was no one, and no glass. In fact, she remembered that Simon hadn't been drinking, which seemed even more curious. Gilly caught up with her friends in the car park.

"Have you found him?" they asked.

"I haven't," Gilly replied.

They said farewell and drove off. Gilly still kept looking as she left the car park. This was a mystery, and she felt rather uneasy. It was as if Simon had never been in the pub at all. The next day at school, Gilly felt grateful for the distraction of her job. She could concentrate on her class, and it wasn't until lunchtime when one of her friends from the previous evening enquired about Simon.

"He's history. Long gone," was Gilly's response, although she knew he was very much on her mind.

Chapter 4

At the weekend, Gilly went to see her mother. It was a Saturday afternoon and Julia wanted to find out what Gilly was planning to do at Christmas.

"Why do you ask?" said Gilly. "You know I'll go and see Daddy, then have lunch with you as usual."

"I thought you might like to spend it with Jimmy," said Julia, peering over her glasses.

"Jimmy is a good friend and that's all it is, thank you," said Gilly firmly. She knew her mother would be delighted if they got together. "Anyway, I met a really good-looking guy in the week."

"Well, tell me more, darling," Julia demanded.

Gilly described Simon and the events of Tuesday evening. Her mother pointed out that Gilly had been very busy lately, and how the mind can play tricks.

"Do you think I imagined him?" asked Gilly.

"Well, if no one else saw him, that could explain things. Or maybe he left while your back was turned."

Gilly thought for a moment. Her mother was right, as usual – Simon must have left as she walked back to join her friends. That put Gilly's mind at ease, and now she could wind down in time for Christmas.

Gilly looked forward to Christmas. Her class usually made presents and decorations, and they were always excited, anticipating what Father Christmas may bring. As usual, the local vicar would come along and give a service.

During the Christmas holidays, many of her friends and her mother were ill, either with colds or flu, so not much happened socially. Gilly was pleased when the new year arrived so she could return to school.

Early in January, while taking a day away from school, Gilly met her mother in Aldbridge. Their local market town was a beautiful place to visit, with a high street full of historic buildings. They enjoyed lunch at a popular café where the staff were friendly and efficient, and the food was excellent. Gilly and her mother always had lunch there when they were in town. The reason for their visit was to go to Lathams, the local saleroom.

Lathams was on the edge of the town in a large redbrick Victorian building. The saleroom was owned by Bishop Donald Latham, and his wife was in charge of the business. As Julia was a friend of Barbara Latham's, she would support her by occasionally purchasing items at auction.

By the time they arrived, the sale had started. Gilly and her mother just about managed to find a seat. Julia thought she might buy some table lamps, which were to be sold later in the auction. It was a good sales day, with most lots fetching good prices.

A new item was announced, and the sales assistant very carefully carried in a doll. The doll was around fourteen inches tall with long, curly brown hair. She wore a maroon dress with a cream cardigan and brown leather shoes.

"I have a lot of interest in this china doll, believed to be German. Very good condition. However, she has a replacement hand," said the auctioneer. "Very rare, I believe," he added.

There were several people bidding in the room and the bids soon reached the high hundreds. Then in came a phone bidder, taking the value into the thousands. Bids in the saleroom stopped, but before long another phone bidder entered the auction. Everyone was amazed as the value rose. The doll sold for six-and-a-half thousand pounds.

Gilly had noticed that a man sitting near her had been bidding for the doll. She overheard him telling the lady next to him, "If the hand was original, the value would double."

Everyone, including Gilly and her mother, started talking about the doll, so it was several minutes before the sale resumed. All the lots were selling, and most were selling for decent money.

"I hope those lamps stay affordable," remarked Julia.

"Are they for you, Mummy?" asked Gilly.

"They're for a customer of mine who couldn't make

it to the sale today," answered Julia. "She has given me a figure to bid up to, so wish me luck!"

The lamps' turn came, and Julia was successful in securing them both. Gilly and her mother left the auction, paying for the lamps and instructing the saleroom to deliver to the address Julia had given. They parted in the car park, promising to catch up at the weekend. They often spent time together, and they were used to people mistaking them for sisters.

For some time, Julia had been giving a lot of thought to her future. Continuing to live in the large farmhouse alone seemed ridiculous. Her husband Charles would be difficult to manage at home, even if he had the right care, and he seemed content where he was. She had thought that if Gilly were to marry, the house could pass to her. It was a good home for raising a family, as she knew. However, there were no signs of this happening.

Their friend Jimmy Shaw had said on many occasions that he could find a much smaller property, or even build one for her so she could have exactly what she wanted. Whatever she decided, things would happen gradually. There was so much to sort out.

Julia made a start in the attic. Items stored away for years could be disposed of, she thought. She did approach Charles for his view of her downsizing, and as usual his reply was, "You must do, as always, just as you like."

She wondered why she bothered. He never cared about anything she did, but at least this approach made things easier for her.

Gilly called round to see her mother the following Saturday afternoon.

"Looks as if you need a skip, Mummy," she remarked. The kitchen table was piled high with boxes and papers.

"Not until I've sorted through everything," replied her mother.

The two of them sat and looked through photo albums. Time passed quickly, and they realised it had grown dark.

"Will you be staying?" asked Julia.

"I might as well now," Gilly replied. She often stayed after evenings with her mother, when she found she had drunk too much gin to drive home safely.

"This is very addictive, looking at the past," commented Gilly. Julia put together a quick meal so they could resume their trip down memory lane. Gilly opened a large cardboard box tied with coloured string. It contained more photos, school books, school reports. Reading the reports amused Gilly, as they were very similar to the ones she was writing herself, although she felt some of comments about her were unfair.

She peered into the box. At the bottom, among pebbles and seashells, was a doll's hand. She lifted it out.

"Do you remember this, Mummy?"

"I do," her mother replied.

"Do you think it's the original hand of the doll we saw at the sale?" Gilly sounded excited.

"Perhaps it is. We could always take it along for someone's opinion," her mother replied.

"We'd better keep it safe. It may be valuable, and we could use some money at school for new gym equipment."

Her mother brought her down to earth, pointing out that it may not be from that particular doll, and that the new owner might only offer a small amount for the hand. Once again, Gilly looked in the box, and found an old grey notepad.

"Oh, yes," she remarked.

"Pardon?" said her mother.

"Do you remember the summer when we didn't have a holiday away?"

"I can, just about. It was a long while ago, darling."

"I wrote a story about that hand," said Gilly, holding up the notebook, "and here it is!"

"Oh, good," her mother replied as she looked at the old photo albums.

Gilly flicked through the pages of the notebook.

"Oh gosh. My description of the doll is the same as the doll at the auction. How odd is that?"

Her mother, still looking at old photos, answered, "Really?"

After a while, Julia, who was engrossed with the old photos, sensed something was wrong. Gilly had laid the notepad on the table and was gazing at the hand beside it. She had lost all her colour and looked white.

"Darling, what's happened?" asked her mother.

"Simon Newton." Gilly replied, passing her mother the notepad. "He's in my story, see?"

Julia read through until she came to Simon Newton.

"Why your concern?" asked Julia.

"Well, Simon is – or was – real. I've even seen him," answered Gilly in a frail voice.

Julia walked to a dresser, opened a drawer, and took out a telephone directory. She sat down and thumbed through the pages.

"Look, there." she said sharply.

Gilly took the book. Her mother's finger was pointing to the name of Newton, in particular 'S. Newton'.

"Perhaps one of these is a Simon Newton. It's not an unusual name."

Her mother's observations were justified and Gilly breathed deeply. Julia reached for the gin and a bottle of tonic, and filled her daughter's glass. They sat for some while in silence, Julia still looking at the photo albums while her daughter sat wondering why she had chosen to write her story with the characters she had.

"Have I convinced you not to make too much of this?"

her mother asked, in a much softer voice.

"I think so," was Gilly's reply. "The drink is certainly helping."

"I think things will seem different after a night's sleep," remarked Julia, as she looked at her watch.

"It is rather late. I'll go up to bed and see you in the morning, Mummy."

Gilly slept very well, which, considering the amount of gin she had consumed, was no great surprise. At breakfast time, both of them were suffering from over-indulging.

By mid-morning Gilly left for home. She didn't take any items from the box, but asked her mother to contact the saleroom regarding the doll's hand. At home, she made herself a snack and filled the afternoon marking her class's work.

Gilly tried to accept her mother's comments regarding Simon Newton, and she took on more work at school. There were plans for the school to re-locate and incorporate a small school from another village. Gilly's headmistress, Angela Summers, had spoken to Gilly, encouraging her to apply for the position of headmistress when the time was right. Miss Summers had plans to retire early, but she would remain in her post until the school moved. She liked Gilly very much, and knew she had the ability to become the new head.

Early the next week, Julia took the doll's hand to

Lathams and left it to be examined by one of their experts. Later that week, she received a call from the saleroom.

The lady who spoke to Julia told her there was very good news regarding the hand, and invited her to pop in in the near future. In the evening, Julia rang her daughter, asking her to be available on Saturday morning to visit the saleroom. Gilly agreed, and the pair arranged to meet at the saleroom at around half-past ten.

Saturday morning came and Gilly arrived ahead of her mother. She parked in the Lathams car park and waited. Julia didn't turn up until around twenty to eleven, but this wasn't unusual, so Gilly didn't moan.

"Good morning, darling," Julia called out as she closed her car door.

Gilly greeted her mother, and the pair entered the sale-room. They made their way to the office.

"I've arranged to meet Barbara Latham," Julia announced.

Barbara was sitting in the office. She was a smallish lady with light, short brown hair, and a very pleasant freck-led face. She wore a loose-fitting brown and cream jumper with black trousers.

"Good to see you, Barbara," Julia said in a soft voice as the pair entered the office.

Barbara, who was sitting behind her desk, stood up and shook Julia's hand.

"You remember Gilly," added Julia.

"Of course I do. Good to see you, Gilly." Barbara held out her hand for Gilly to take.

"Thank you for seeing us this morning," said Gilly as they all sat down.

"Now, regarding your hand. Our expert has confirmed he is almost certain that it belongs to the rare doll we sold recently. I have made contact with the buyer, who is delighted the original hand has been located. While you're here I shall call the new owner, so you can make the necessary arrangements for him to see the hand and negotiate with you."

"Is the doll's owner someone you know?" asked Julia.

"We do notify him when we sell collectors' dolls," replied Barbara.

"So, he has bought from you before?"

"He has," said Barbara. "He is a Doctor Ian McGregor, and he lives in Carlisle."

Julia looked at Gilly as Barbara pulled the phone towards her.

"Shall I call him?" asked Barbara.

"Please do," replied Gilly.

It seemed a little while before the call was answered.

"Good morning, Ian. It's Barbara Latham calling regarding your doll's missing hand." Barbara seemed very friendly towards him. "May I pass you over to the owner, a Miss Raymond?" she asked. Barbara held the receiver for

Gilly to take.

"Good morning, Doctor McGregor," said Gilly, politely.

"Please, call me Ian," replied Doctor McGregor in a soft voice.

"Very well, Ian. I'm Gilly."

"Excellent. I feel we already have a connection, with the doll belonging to both of us," said Ian.

"Indeed. However, the pieces surely belong together," replied Gilly.

"May I ask something of you, Gilly?" Ian said. "I definitely want to purchase the hand from you, but I won't be able to collect it myself. The doll is of great interest to me, and I don't want the hand to be sent by mail or delivery service. So, if I send you money for the rail fare, would you deliver it in person? Please, come and spend a long weekend with myself and my wife."

"May I take a little time to consider this, Ian?"

"As long as you need," said Ian. "I'm very patient."

"Thank you. If it's convenient, I'll call you later," replied Gilly.

"That's fine. Barbara will give you my details, so I'll look forward to hearing from you. It's been a pleasure talking to you, Gilly. Goodbye for now."

Gilly returned the receiver to Barbara, who replaced it on the phone. Both her mother and Barbara looked at her expectantly.

"Ian would like me to deliver the hand in person. He is unable to travel, and doesn't want to use the post or couriers. He offered to cover my travel costs, and he invited me to stay for a long weekend with him and his wife."

"So, when he purchased the doll from you, Barbara, what arrangements were made then?" enquired Julia.

"Well, Ian has a friend who was visiting the area shortly after the sale, and was able to collect the doll on his behalf. He has in the past been able to collect items himself. However, he does suffer with his back, and he can't travel far at present."

"May I take Ian's contact details so I can make arrangements a little later?" asked Gilly.

Barbara wrote Ian's details on a card and added, "Ian is a lovely man. You will be safe and very well looked after, I can assure you both of that."

Gilly and her mother left the saleroom. Gilly sat in her mother's car to discuss Ian's request.

After a short conversation, they both decided she should contact Ian and make arrangements for her visit. A couple of years earlier, Gilly had travelled to Newcastle to attend a course with some other teachers, so the rail journey didn't concern her. Because Barbara had given them assurance of Ian's background, they were both satisfied she would be in good hands.

Later that afternoon, Gilly rang Ian and arranged to visit

during the half-term break. Her school would close for the week in mid-February, and this year it was closing on the Thursday for boiler repairs to be carried out on Friday. Gilly arranged to travel on the Friday, spend three nights with the McGregors, and return on the Monday. Ian was delighted, and promised to post the rail tickets. He was very much looking forward to meeting her.

By the middle of the following week, Gilly had received her rail tickets. Ian had written a lovely letter saying he was so grateful to her for taking the trouble to trace the doll's whereabouts, and for agreeing to deliver the hand in person. He had also sent a cheque, and explained she must use this for refreshments during her journey.

Chapter 5

Gilly was looking forward to her visit and meeting the McGregors, so when the Friday morning arrived, she was up very early. She was due to catch the train at six o'clock from Ipswich station. The journey should take around eight hours and, as she remembered, she would have to change trains at Peterborough and again at Newcastle, before finally arriving at Carlisle at around two in the afternoon.

She had wondered how she would pass the time on the journey, and decided against marking some school work, just in case anything was lost. Instead, she packed some magazines and books, which would keep her entertained en route.

Gilly was taking her large travelling carpet bag. It held everything she needed for a weekend visit. Between her clothes, books, and magazines, carefully wrapped in cloths and an old t-shirt, was the doll's hand.

Gilly was ready when her mother arrived to collect her. Julia drove a large Volvo estate, so Gilly's bag fitted easily on the back seats.

"I'm looking forward to this weekend," said Gilly.

Her mother gave a loud yawn. "Rather you than me," she replied. "I think I'll be going back to bed after I've dropped you off."

Gilly knew her mother wasn't an early morning person, but Julia had insisted on taking her to the station. Julia dropped her daughter outside the station, and Gilly grabbed her bag and kissed her mother goodbye.

Gilly walked through the station entrance. There were already several people there, but then it was a weekday. A train was waiting on the platform.

"Is this the six o'clock for Peterborough?" she asked a porter as she passed.

"It is, Miss," he replied.

Gilly found her carriage and made her way to her seat. She took two magazines from her bag before carefully placing it above her head on the luggage rack. Her seat was by the window, which was good, and by the time the train pulled out of the station, no one had taken the seat next to her.

The first part of her journey was pleasant. Sitting alone reading, time passed quickly, and although the train stopped several times, no one who boarded asked if they might sit next to her. On arrival at Peterborough station, Gilly enquired about the departure time of the train to Newcastle. There was time for her to pop into the station café and have a drink. Gilly always welcomed a cup of fresh-brewed tea.

She grabbed her bag and headed for the platform, after checking that the train was ready for boarding. She walked through her carriage and found her seat. Once again, the seat was by a window, and airline-style, so no one could sit opposite.

Gilly took another magazine from her bag before lifting it onto the luggage rack. The carriage was nearly full, but once again she was sitting alone when the train pulled out of the station. She noticed there had been a shower of rain, but the sky looked lighter and she hoped the weekend weather would be settled. She had started to read her magazine when the conductor asked to see her ticket. Gilly reached in her jacket pocket and gave it to the young-looking man.

"Thank you, Miss," he said, and moved along.

Gilly found herself distracted by the changing landscape, and the larger towns and cities along the route. The carriage remained busy, and between stations the seat next to her became occupied. An older lady, very well-dressed and well-spoken, asked if she could join her.

Gilly agreed. They commented on the weather, then Gilly returned to her magazine. The lady next to her took a book from her bag and started to read.

Gilly wondered what life would be like living in these large cities. She supposed it would be more exciting than rural East Anglia, with plenty going on, but Gilly enjoyed life as it was, and had always been content with the rather laid-back Suffolk lifestyle.

The train drew into Newcastle and she wondered whether she would have time for a bite to eat in one of the station cafés. She did manage to have a quick coffee and a sausage roll before boarding the train to Carlisle. This time the seat was facing another pair of seats. The carriage wasn't busy so she laid her bag on the seat opposite. She had one more magazine to read, but because she hadn't been to this area before, she decided to spend her time watching the landscape from the window.

The journey passed quickly, and as the train pulled into Carlisle, she glanced at her watch. It was around quarter to two. Gilly opened her bag and slid her magazine inside. Ian had given brief directions to his home, but he had assumed Gilly would take a taxi.

After leaving the train, she made her way through the station and towards the taxi rank. Although the afternoon was cold and overcast, it was dry with a strong breeze. Good conditions for her to stretch her legs, she thought. She approached a taxi, but only to ask for directions. The rather overweight taxi driver gave her a good idea where to go in a northern accent. She thanked him and headed in the direction he had pointed.

The McGregors lived on Victoria Place. The taxi driver estimated it as a half-mile walk from the station. She reached a stone wall the taxi driver had mentioned, which would take her into an old churchyard, and cut off a corner from her route. Walking along, the steps he had told her about appeared. She made her way up carefully, as they seemed well-worn and slippery.

As she reached the top she looked back. She found herself high up, with good views towards the station. She continued along the gravel pathway towards the church, which appeared to be closed, with some of the windows boarded up. Gilly noticed a wooden bench opposite a side path to the church. She put her bag down and took a brief rest. The church was built from stone, and somewhat discoloured through age, but the boards covering the windows had a newish appearance. Maybe some idiot had smashed them on purpose.

Gilly's eyes were drawn to a gravestone at the opposite end of the church, at the side of the path. There seemed to be a light shining on the gravestone. She looked up at the sky for a break in the clouds, but the day was still grey and overcast. She lowered her head and peered at the gravestone, and again saw a light shining upon it. At first, she wanted to walk down the path and see why this was.

No, she thought. *What if someone is there, and this is a trap for a woman on her own?*

That made her feel uneasy, so she stood up, threw her bag over her shoulder and carried on along the main pathway. When she reached the exit, she turned and looked back, but the gravestone was out of sight.

The taxi driver's directions were exact. Opposite the wide road outside the churchyard was the sign for Victoria Place. She was looking for number ten, but the numbers here were high, so she still had some ground to cover. The houses were all large, and many dated from the Victorian era, built from red brick and very neat. As the numbers decreased, she found herself standing at some tall iron gates. The gates were open and, as the previous house displayed the number twelve, she reasoned that this must be number ten.

Gilly walked through the gates onto a short tarmac drive leading to a garage. The house was a good size, but not as huge as some she had passed. Once again, it was a red brick Victorian property with bay windows and a lovely stained-glass pane in the front door. Her eyes were drawn to the well-kept front garden, and the trees and shrubs blocking the view of the houses opposite. She turned her head and pressed the bell. Gilly could see a figure behind the stained glass, and then the door opened.

"Hello, Gilly. Welcome. I'm Ian," said the man.

He wasn't at all as Gilly had imagined. He was much older than he sounded over the phone – a man well into his sixties, of slight build, with short, greyish hair and beard. He wore glasses, and behind those a very kind smile on his face.

"Good afternoon, Ian. It's a pleasure to meet you,"

Gilly said, holding out her hand for Ian to shake.

"Please come in. My wife Audrey is keen to meet you too. She'll be down shortly."

She stepped into the wide hallway, admiring the lovely tiled floor. Ian directed Gilly to her right and into a well-furnished lounge at the front of the house.

"Please take a seat and rest your bag somewhere," he suggested.

As Gilly sat, and before Ian could say another word, she heard footsteps on the stairs. Ian moved slightly and Audrey entered.

"Good afternoon, Gilly. Lovely to meet you!"

Audrey approached with open arms, so Gilly stood up. Audrey gave her a hug. She was a tall, slender woman with dark brown hair in a bob. She appeared to be much younger than Ian.

"Has Ian offered you a drink?" Audrey asked, and Gilly shook her head. "Well, come along, Doctor," Audrey commanded. "A tray of drinks for us all! What would you prefer, Gilly?"

"Tea would be lovely, please," replied Gilly.

With that, Ian left the room. There was no doubt who was in charge here.

"How was your journey?" Audrey asked.

Gilly gave an account of the journey and her day so far, but made no mention of the light she had seen in the churchyard. Ian returned after a short while with a tray of cups and saucers, teapot, milk jug and sugar bowl, in a lovely green-coloured china. He rested the tray on a low table between her armchair and the sofa opposite, where Audrey was sitting. When Ian had poured the tea, he was just about to sit on the sofa when Audrey enquired as to the whereabouts of the cake. Ian once more left the room.

"I do like my slice of cake in the afternoon. I thought after all these years Doctor Ian might just have remembered!" said Audrey, disapprovingly.

Ian returned. He made an excellent cup of tea, and the cake was delicious.

"What good fortune that you attended the auction and recognised the doll, Gilly!" Audrey commented.

"Well, it was only when my mother was sorting out some things from the attic, and found a box containing some of my childhood treasures, that I made the connection. The saleroom manager was certain the hand had once belonged to the doll."

Gilly reached for her bag and started to look for the prized hand. She noticed Ian had edged forward on the sofa, and was eagerly waiting to see what she had brought. She located the t-shirt containing the hand and unwrapped it from the cloths, then passed it over to Ian. His face was beaming. It was as if he was a child at Christmas.

"Gilly, I can't thank you enough. I am certain this is her

missing hand." He carefully passed the hand to Audrey, who gave an approving smile. "May I show you my collection?" said Ian, as he looked enthusiastically at Gilly.

"Please do." Gilly replied.

"I'll see to our dinner while you're shown the prize collection," said Audrey.

Gilly followed Ian as he made his way upstairs. She thought the house was immaculate and the paintings on the wall were superb. Ian made his way along the landing.

"Before you meet the dolls, I should show you your room. I hope you'll make yourself at home in here," said Ian as he opened a bedroom door. The room was above the lounge, with a large window. The double bed looked luxurious, the soft pile of the carpet moulded around her feet, the walls looked freshly painted in a pale shade of pink, and more paintings furnished the walls.

"Do you paint, Ian?" asked Gilly.

"Only the walls. Audrey is the artist. Do you like her work?" he asked.

"Yes, I do," she replied enthusiastically. The paintings featured landscapes from the Lake District, as well as local buildings, seascapes, and gardens, some in oil, some watercolour. They really were works of art. Ian assured Gilly that Audrey would tell her all about the paintings over the weekend. She could see he was keen to show her his collection of dolls.

"Would you like to meet the ladies?" he asked.

"Yes, please," Gilly replied. "I'm looking forward to seeing your collection."

Gilly followed Ian from her room and along the landing to a room at the back of the house. Ian opened the door for Gilly and announced, "We have a visitor, girls."

Gilly walked into the large room. There were glass-fronted wooden cabinets along the left-hand side, and to the right were two smaller, free-standing cabinets. She was expecting the collection to be much larger, with dolls everywhere. However, these were tastefully arranged, with many dolls sitting or lying down. She noticed that the condition of every doll was perfect, as she had expected.

"What a wonderful collection! Have you been collecting for some while?"

Ian closed the door.

"Please sit down," he said, as he directed his hand towards a sofa. They sat, and Ian revealed that he and Audrey had started the collection when they discovered it wouldn't be possible for them to have children. "These have become our family, really," he explained. "They are all great characters, and they still bring a tremendous amount of pleasure to us both."

This wasn't what Gilly had expected, and she found his revelation slightly creepy.

"How many girls do you have then, Ian?"

"We have seventy, now that we've acquired Bedina," replied Ian.

"That's an unusual name," said Gilly, wondering why it sounded familiar.

Ian stood up and walked to a cabinet behind the sofa. She could hear the door open, and a moment later he returned to sit beside her with the doll she had seen at the auction.

"Do they all have names?" she asked.

"Oh, yes. We name them all."

The doll was sitting on his knee as he stroked its hair. He reached into his waistcoat pocket and produced the hand. He carefully examined the hand and looked at the false hand. He explained that someone had carved a wooden replacement hand, and that it had been done exceptionally well. He would replace this with the original, and keep the carved one to remind him of how she had arrived.

"Do you repair them yourself?" asked Gilly.

"I can fit new hands, feet and limbs. I repair ceramics, replace hair and repair damaged paintwork. Audrey can make new clothes if required. However, these will all need to be identical to the originals," Ian explained. "Would you care to hold her, Gilly?" he asked.

Gilly hesitated.

Should I, or shouldn't I?

She pushed the strange thought away, held out her hands and gently took the doll. She had an attractive face, much kinder-looking than others in the collection.

"She is beautiful, Ian, and so lucky to have found such a caring home."

"Yes, she is, and she deserves some happiness. I can't help feeling that if she could talk to us, she might reveal a very disturbing history."

Ian looked troubled.

"Do you mean when her hand was broken?" asked Gilly.

"I feel that something happened after that. Something really disturbing and troubling. Something I suspect we shall never know," said Ian.

Gilly passed the doll back to Ian.

How could he know such things about the doll's past? she wondered. Perhaps it would be better not to ask.

Ian took the doll, replaced her on a chair in the cabinet, and closed the door.

"Shall we go down for dinner?" he suggested.

"Yes, please," Gilly replied. It had been a long day, and she was ready for a hot meal.

Audrey was in the kitchen as the passed, and Ian enquired if he could help. His offer was declined and Audrey suggested he should keep Gilly company in the dining room.

The dining room was opposite the lounge, the table laid ready for the meal. Gilly noticed more paintings on the wall, as well as cabinets displaying a fine collection of china. Ian pulled a chair away from the table, and asked Gilly to please be seated, before sitting opposite her himself. Before she could comment on the china, Audrey came in with a large casserole dish and placed it on the table.

"I do hope chicken casserole will be acceptable for you," said Audrey, as she sat to Gilly's left.

The casserole was excellent. Audrey could certainly cook. Dinner seemed to last for ages, with good wine and a selection of desserts. Gilly felt full and really looked after. They stayed sitting at the table, chatting about Audrey's love of painting, and how she had studied art at university in her youth. Gilly discovered Audrey was a librarian at the University of Carlisle.

Before clearing the table, Ian returned to the subject of the doll's hand, and spoke of the payment he would make. Gilly thanked him, although a figure had yet to be agreed. Ian asked whether she had any plans for the money.

"Oh, yes," she replied. "I plan to put the funds towards some new gym equipment for the school where I work. It's something we really need."

"I see," said Ian. There was a long pause as he ran his fingers through his beard. "Then, in that case, I will double the amount I will be giving you, Gilly."

"Well, thank you very much. That is really kind of you, and will be greatly appreciated."

As yet, Ian hadn't mentioned a figure, and Gilly realised

she had expressed her gratitude before knowing the amount.

"Does a thousand pounds sound acceptable?" asked Ian.

Gilly was taken aback at the amount he was offering. This far exceeded the figure she had in mind.

"Are you really sure, Ian? That does sound very generous."

"I am very happy with the figure, and I shall write a cheque before you leave us on Monday."

Audrey suggested that Gilly and herself should retire to the lounge while Ian cleared the table. Gilly offered to help, only to be met with a "Certainly not!" from Audrey. "You are our guest, and I have cooked the dinner. Therefore it is Doctor Ian's turn to assist."

The pair stood up and headed for the lounge, leaving Ian collecting plates to be taken to the kitchen. There would be no arguing with Audrey.

They made themselves comfortable in the lounge, and Audrey made some suggestions as to how they might spend tomorrow. After a while, Ian appeared and asked if any more drinks were needed. However, his offer was declined, and soon afterwards they all left for bed.

Chapter 6

Saturday morning was very bright and breezy. Gilly had slept well after her long day. She knew relaxing in bed for long would be difficult, as her hosts had plans to show her their home city. She could hear Ian and Audrey downstairs, so it was time for her to make a move. She washed and dressed for breakfast. The smell of bacon told her the day was off to a good start.

After breakfast, she could tell Ian and Audrey were keen to make a move, so she quickly got ready.

Ian's car wasn't as Gilly had expected. She knew her father liked Jaguars and Daimlers when he could still drive, and her mother loved her Volvos. Ian and Audrey shared a car – a Honda, and not a recent one. Ian parked outside a friend's house in the centre of Carlisle.

Audrey was keen for Gilly to visit the cathedral. This was an excellent choice, as Gilly was very keen on history. According to Audrey, it was the second smallest cathedral in England.

Inside, the bright sunlight poured through the great East window. There was so much to see! Ian drifted off on his own while Gilly and Audrey took in the many amazing features of the cathedral. Gilly was keen to visit the shop so she could buy a guide book and postcards for her class, to show them where she had been.

They met up with Ian, who was examining the painted panels on the back of the choir stalls. Audrey looked at her watch, and suggested they should go and have some lunch. As they walked away from the cathedral, Gilly turned around to look at the building. The stone was a lovely bronze colour in the sunlight, and the tower looked far less imposing than it would if it had had a huge spire.

Audrey knew a small restaurant nearby, so it was there that they would have their lunch. After an excellent meal, which Gilly was treated to, they made their way to the city centre for a look around the shops. Time soon passed, and Ian said he would like to head for home. Audrey gave a sigh.

"Can't you keep up with the youth of today, Doctor?" She could be very sarcastic to her husband when she wanted to be.

"And where might they be, then?" replied Ian.

Gilly had to smile, and was glad he had retaliated. They headed for the car and made their way home. Once again, Gilly asked whether she could help, and again her offer was declined.

After a superb tea, Gilly sat talking to Ian. For the first time, he revealed that he was a botanist. Gilly found him very interesting to talk to. With her mother being a florist, she could relate to plants and flowers. He told her that on Sunday morning he would show her around the large back garden, which she had only glimpsed from indoors.

The evening passed very quickly, and when Audrey joined them, she soon authorised drinks to be served. Gilly attempted to consume only small amounts of gin and tonic, which proved to be difficult as Ian constantly filled her glass.

The next morning, Gilly was surprised not to have more of a headache. As before, she could hear Ian and Audrey downstairs, so she felt it was time to join them. Breakfast was light, as Audrey informed her there would be a large roast lunch to look forward to.

"I am hoping Ian will be able to entertain you this morning," Audrey said, as she looked at her husband.

"I shall be happy to," replied Ian.

Gilly was looking forward to seeing the garden and, as the weather was again sunny and bright, this would be the ideal opportunity. After breakfast, Gilly went to the bathroom to freshen up and put on some warmer clothes. She made her way downstairs to the hall, where she was met by Ian. He was wearing a dark green jacket with endless pockets.

"Are you dressed for gardening?" asked Gilly.

"Perhaps I am! However, I was only going to show you the gardens, and yes, this is my gardening coat," Ian replied softly.

They left the house through the kitchen door, to the

rear of the property. The garden was mature and densely planted with interesting trees and shrubs. They walked on the well-kept lawn. Gilly could recognise many of the trees and plants, and for the ones she didn't know, Ian was very pleased to go into great detail about their names and origins. The garden, which was partly walled, seemed to be much larger than the gardens of the other houses, which Gilly mentioned to Ian.

"That's right. We do have a large garden. Shortly after we moved here there was a spare plot of land where we are now. This came onto the market with outline permission for another house. I purchased it immediately and transformed it into the garden," said Ian, proudly.

"That was an excellent idea. You had great vision," Gilly replied.

The garden was divided into different areas, separated by neatly clipped hedges.

"Please tell me if I'm boring you, Gilly," said Ian, who was going into great detail about the more unusual plants.

"I'm finding your knowledge fascinating," Gilly assured him. "I so wish I had a garden of my own. Somewhere I could escape to."

Gilly thought the garden was marvellous, and was keen to explore it all. Ian glanced at his watch.

"I think we should make our way back for lunch," he said.

"Is it really that time already?"

"Yes. The morning has passed too soon. I do hope you've enjoyed our garden."

Gilly thanked him very much. She would love to have continued the tour after lunch, but something else was on her mind. The brightly lit gravestone in the churchyard had been in her thoughts since Friday, and she was eager to return and hopefully find out why.

Audrey's lunch was superb. The rib of beef melted in the mouth and her potatoes were the best Gilly had ever tasted – crunchy and golden, and soft and flowery inside. Audrey revealed that over the years she had hosted endless dinner parties, and was keen to excel for her guests. For dessert, she served a mouth-watering sherry trifle, as this was Ian's favourite.

As usual, after lunch it was Ian's task to clean up, and before Audrey could escort her to the lounge Gilly said, "I'd like to go out for a walk this afternoon, if that's alright."

Gilly wondered whether Audrey would ask to join her. She didn't want to appear rude by saying she wanted to go alone.

"You go off and enjoy yourself, Gilly. I'll see that Ian sorts things out here, and on your return, we'll have a drink."

Gilly made her way into the hall. She had left her jacket over the banister, and quickly slipped it on.

"I shall see you both later, then," she said as she approached the front door.

Gilly headed in the direction she had walked from on Friday. The afternoon was bright, and not so windy as the morning. She walked quickly, eager to reach the church-yard and find out why the light had been shining on the headstone. Once in the churchyard, she could see people attending to the graves with flowers and water. This gave Gilly peace of mind, knowing she wasn't there alone.

She reached the bench where she had rested on Friday, and again she sat for a moment. She found herself looking down the path to the side of the church, and on towards the gravestone. She could see no light on it today, but the day was so bright that another light wouldn't be seen. She stood up and slowly walked along the path, stopping behind the gravestone for a while, looking around to see whether there were any lights from the church pointing in her direction. There were none.

Gilly took a few more steps and turned around to look at the front of the gravestone. Her eyes focused on the names engraved. She read, *John Ross Newton and Margaret New-ton. Tragically taken before their time. Loving parents to Simon. May they rest in peace.*

Gilly stood back from the grave and leant against the church wall. She was breathing deeply and feeling very disturbed. For a moment, she closed her eyes. She told herself she was mistaken, that the names were similar to the ones she had created as a child, and that when her eyes were open again the names would be slightly different.

Slowly her eyes opened, peering at the gravestone. The names remained the same. She felt extremely uneasy. She turned away and walked quickly to the bench on the main path, and sat down. She was still breathing quickly.

The light on the gravestone when she arrived had been meant to draw her here. She was meant to come to Carlisle to see this. Gilly had been convinced by her mother that she had imagined meeting Simon, knowing he had featured in her story, written when she was a child – but now it all seemed real.

Why? she thought. *Why?*

Perhaps now, with the doll complete, this would end. Maybe it would all be over … but she just knew there would be more to come.

Gilly told herself she must continue her walk, return to the McGregors, and try to appear calm. She was breathing more easily now, but noticed her hands were shaking. She stood up, tempted to return to the grave.

No, she must resist and walk away.

After leaving the churchyard, she remembered the route Ian had taken in the car yesterday. She could walk back to their home in a more roundabout way, perhaps giving her enough time to compose herself. As she walked, she thought perhaps the McGregors might have some distant memories about the Newton's accident. After all, they had lived here for a long time.

On second thoughts, she decided not to mention any of this. All she had to do was to appear to be her usual self. This would not be easy, and she could still feel her hands shaking as she approached their house.

Gilly was making her way towards the front door as it opened. Ian was waiting to greet her.

"Have you enjoyed your stroll around the neighbourhood?"

"I have, thank you," replied Gilly. She stepped into the hallway as Ian closed the door.

"Please come in and sit down," said Ian as he ushered her into the lounge.

Audrey was reading the newspaper. "Are you alright?" she asked. "Come and sit down!"

They could tell something was wrong. The concerned looks on their faces meant that Gilly would need to give some explanation.

"My dear, you seem very nervous and all your colour has disappeared. Whatever has happened?" asked Audrey.

Dismissing their concerns was not an option, and Gilly found herself giving an explanation.

"I was walking through the churchyard at the end of the road, as I did on Friday. When I was leaving, my foot slipped on the steps. I didn't fall as such, but I feel extremely shaken. I managed to hold onto the handrail, which saved me."

Audrey was looking at Ian. Gilly knew neither of them was convinced, but this was all she was prepared to tell them.

"Ian, will you make Gilly one of your herbal teas?" suggested Audrey.

Ian left the room. Audrey changed the subject and talked about some article she was reading in the paper, although Gilly wasn't really paying much attention. And why was she being offered herbal tea? She had tried herbal teas in the past, but they were not to her liking.

Ian seemed to be gone for ages, and Gilly was offered the newspaper supplement by Audrey. She was flicking through without much interest when Ian finally appeared with a tray containing three cups and saucers. He placed it on the table and passed a cup to Gilly first.

"Thank you, Ian," she said as she took a small sip.

The tea tasted better than she expected, although it was rather sweet. They all sat in silence for a while looking through the papers. Gilly began to feel more relaxed. The Newtons' grave was still on her mind, but not dominating her thoughts as before.

Ian spoke first, asking Gilly if she was looking forward to returning home. Gilly answered that she was looking forward to seeing her mother and then catching up on her class's work from school before term resumed next week. Audrey suggested preparing some tea, but Gilly declined anything more to eat, saying she was still full after that lovely lunch.

"Will you have an early night, Gilly?" asked Ian.

"I think I must, with the early start I need to make," she replied.

"Would you like to say farewell to the girls?" said Ian.

Gilly thought for a moment. The Girls. *Oh, the dolls!* It had better be a 'yes', as he would be offended if she declined.

"I would love to," she said.

Chapter 7

Gilly still felt dazed from her unusual drink. She could see that Ian, who was now standing, was keen to make a move. He gathered the cups and saucers onto the tray and headed for the kitchen.

"Go on then, Gilly. Say your goodbyes," said Audrey as she raised her eyebrows.

Gilly stood up and headed for the hall, where she was met by Ian.

"After you," he said. She headed up the stairs.

Ian went into the dolls' room first, turned on the light and drew the curtains. She focused on his latest doll and then glanced around to the others.

"They have all enjoyed your company, Gilly, as have Audrey and myself. We hope you'll return and visit us again."

"I would like that very much," replied Gilly. "Both you and Audrey have been excellent hosts, and I couldn't have been looked after better."

Ian opened a drawer at the bottom of the cabinet, picked up an envelope and handed it to Gilly.

"I have already written your cheque," he said, "and I'd like to thank you once again for making Bedina complete.

Please check the amount."

Gilly opened the envelope, and yes, the amount was correct. She thanked Ian very much. On leaving the room she looked once more at Bedina and remembered Ian's comments about her disturbing past. She felt a chill as she said goodbye, remembering her uneasy visit to the Newtons' grave.

The evening passed quickly. Gilly took a quick shower before being served ordinary tea and cake. As she lay in bed, her afternoon seemed unreal. When she thought about looking into the doll's eyes, she knew there would be more uneasy times ahead.

Gilly slept well, only to be woken by a knock on the bedroom door. She could hear Audrey's voice telling her it was time to make a move. She quickly washed and dressed and made her way down for breakfast. As before, a large cooked breakfast was waiting.

"How are you feeling this morning, Gilly?" asked Ian.

"I'm fine, thank you. I slept very well."

"Have you recovered from your near miss yesterday afternoon?" said Audrey with a concerned look.

"I'm much better," Gilly responded. "Especially with the effects of Ian's herbal tea."

"Ian will make a small flask for your journey, but only if you're not going to drive," said Audrey.

Gilly assured her she wouldn't be driving, as her mother would collect her from the station. She was pleased to accept the flask, as the effects of yesterday's beverage had passed and the mystery of the gravestone still weighed heavy on her mind.

It was Ian who drove Gilly to the station. Audrey would like to have seen her off, but she wanted to sort out Gilly's room before going to work. Audrey gave her a big hug and asked her to give them a call when she arrived home. Ian escorted Gilly to the train, and once again he thanked her for the hand, and for personally delivering it to him. She shook his hand and thanked him for an interesting weekend.

"When you find yourself thinking of events from yesterday afternoon, and they are causing you to worry, you must use your flask," Ian said in a soft voice.

"I shall," Gilly replied. "Thank you for your concern."

She made her way through the carriage to find her seat, and once again it was by a window. She placed her bag on the luggage rack and placed the small flask between her handbag and the side of the seat. There were several passengers already on board, but the carriage wasn't full and again she was sitting alone.

She could see Ian waving goodbye as the train left the station. His comments regarding yesterday afternoon and the flask of tea told her that they knew something was wrong in her life, but she decided it was her problem to face alone, and she should be able to cope.

Audrey had given her some magazines that she thought

might interest Gilly for her journey home. Gilly had packed them in her bag, and planned to browse through them after she changed trains at Newcastle. For the moment, she looked through the carriage window as the morning was growing light.

She was thinking about her weekend. In spite of the long journey, it had been enjoyable, and the weather had been kind for her. She thought of Ian and his prized collection of dolls. They were more than just dolls, though. They were his girls – his daughters. Good heavens, he would never manage to father seventy daughters! She managed a weak smile and a silent laugh to herself.

Her thoughts turned to Audrey. She was great. Gilly felt as if she had known her for ages, and oh, how she teased poor Ian! When he responded, his remarks were ten times more penetrating, but they seemed to have no effect on Audrey's mood. Gilly could see that they both enjoyed finding out who would land the fatal blow.

Carlisle had been very interesting, and there would be plenty to tell her class about when school resumed after half term.

Finally, her thoughts turned to yesterday afternoon. Perhaps she should have mentioned the gravestone to Ian. He may have been able to shed some light on what was going on in her life. After all, he was a clever man – but that didn't stop him believing the dolls were his children.

Perhaps she should phone later and explain why she was so shaken. After all, neither of them believed her account of slipping on the steps.

The first part of her journey passed quickly, and as the train eased into Newcastle, she felt the need to use the flask Ian had provided. There was no need to have any food, as her breakfast would keep her going all day.

Before she boarded the train for the next stage of her journey, she made a visit to the toilets for a freshen-up. It was then she noticed her hands shaking, as they had the previous afternoon. She took a deep breath, put her bag, which contained the flask, on her shoulder, and headed onto the platform to find her carriage. Before the train started to move, Gilly poured herself a cup full of Ian's tea. It did have a peculiar aroma and a rather sweet, pleasant taste. She had positioned herself by a window again without really checking the seat number. As the carriage filled up, she realised her seat was actually the one in front. With her tea finished, she thrust the flask in the bag and moved to the seat ahead.

After taking a magazine from her bag, she replaced it once more on the luggage rack. As before, a little while after her drink she felt herself beginning to relax. She could see the conductor approaching. *Good*, she thought, after he had seen and punched her ticket. She could doze for a while.

Gilly noticed that a lady sitting diagonally across the carriage was looking in her direction. She was middle-aged with greying hair and a kind face. Suddenly she stood up and approached Gilly with a pleasant smile.

"Would you care for some company?" the lady asked.

"Please don't think I'm being rude, but at the moment I'm not very good company at all. But thank you for your offer," Gilly politely replied.

The lady returned to her seat and Gilly drifted off to sleep. The next thing she could remember was being woken by the lady who had spoken earlier. She was touching her arm and asking if she needed to change trains. Gilly realised the train had stopped and at Peterborough station. She had slept deeply and was still dazed from her beverage. With her bag on her shoulder, she said thank you and goodbye to the grey-haired lady, and made her way towards the next train for the final part of her journey.

Gilly knew for the last part of the journey she would need to stay awake. She would give her mother a call to come and collect her nearer to home. Feeling calmer and a little more with it, she managed to read one of the magazines from Audrey. Through the window, the sky looked a little brighter here in Suffolk. The train made an extended stop at Bury St Edmunds, so Gilly thought this would be a good time to call her mother. Julia asked her to wait in the café at Ipswich if she wasn't on the platform. That done, she returned to her seat.

Arriving at Ipswich station, she tried to spot her mother,

as not many people were on the platform. No, she wasn't there. The train stopped, Gilly stood up, collected her bag and made for the doors. She made her way towards the café, only to bump into her mother before she could go inside.

"Would you like a drink, darling, before we drive back?" said Julia, giving Gilly a big hug. Gilly declined, suggesting they should head for home.

It was Julia who did most of the talking on the way home, and it was only when they finally sat down at the kitchen table that Gilly was able to give an account of the weekend. She decided not to mention the strange light on the gravestone, and finding out it was the Newtons' grave, until later.

Gilly asked to use the phone to call the McGregors as she had promised. It was Ian who answered. He was pleased to hear she had arrived home safely and thanked her for calling.

When she returned to the kitchen table, Julia commented on her new flask. Gilly took the flask from her bag and placed it on the table.

"Ian made some herbal tea for me to enjoy on the way home."

"I wasn't aware you liked herbal tea," replied Julia.

Now would be a good time to reveal how the drink had helped to calm her. Before she could speak, Julia removed the cup and stopper, placed her nose over the top and inhaled.

"Gosh, it's like … well … like marijuana. Why would he make you tea containing this?" Julia asked, concerned.

"Perhaps you might let me explain," replied Gilly.

Chapter 8

Gilly gave her mother an account of the light on the headstone, and what had happened when she returned to the churchyard to find out who was buried there. She told her mother how she had returned to the house, and what she said to the McGregors. By now Gilly was beginning to feel disturbed again. The effects of the tea were wearing off.

Julia's elbows were on the table with her face resting in her hands. She had listened in silence, looking, emotionless, at her daughter. Finally she gave a sigh.

"If what you've written in your story has actually happened, so what? You met a Simon Newton. You told me how charming he was. You found a doll's hand, which has now been reunited with the doll, and now you are considerably better off. On spending the weekend in Carlisle your attention has been drawn to a grave, the grave of Simon's parents. These things might be strange, but don't let them control you. Take back control of your life, girl!"

Julia spoke very firmly. Gilly had never heard her mother speak to her so forcefully. There was a long silence while she digested her mother's words. Her mother believed her – something she was not expecting – and her advice about taking control of the situation seemed such an easy thing to ask.

Gilly looked into her mother's eyes.

"I'll try to do as you say. After all, Ian is no danger. No harm has come to me. I'll focus on my life and, should anything else come to light, once again I will pull myself together and move on."

Julia was pleased with her daughter's response, and suggested she should stay for the evening. Gilly felt better. It was much easier now that her mother believed her, rather than using coincidences to explain things. She knew if something else were to happen, her mother would be here to listen.

The remainder of the day passed quickly, and Gilly realised she was very tired. Her mother insisted she had an early night. She slept much better than expected, and lay in on the following morning. After a light breakfast, she collected her bag and went to say goodbye.

Julia was in the barn working on a flower arrangement.

"I'm about to leave, Mummy."

Julia left her flowers and walked with Gilly to her car. "I'll lock up and drive you home then."

On the drive home, Julia asked after her daughter's state of mind following their talk the previous evening. Gilly replied that at the moment she was feeling much more level-headed about life than she had for some while. Julia was pleased to hear this, but she assured her daughter that if something else strange were to happen, she would be there for her.

After her mother had dropped her off, Gilly unpacked her bag and placed her cheque on the coffee table in the lounge. She would need to go to the bank later in the week.

The rest of the day Gilly spent relaxing. She would return to going through her class's work and planning their future lessons from tomorrow.

Gilly planned to go shopping on Friday for her groceries, and at the same time pop into the bank and deposit her cheque. Maybe in the afternoon she would have time to visit her father in his exclusive nursing home. She knew she should go and visit him more often, but since his accident he had become very moody, and they usually ended up having an argument. He had never accepted her decision to teach rather than becoming a lawyer, so she could one day take over his practice.

It was on Thursday evening that she sat in her lounge reading through the magazines Audrey had given her to read. She was startled by an unexpected knock on the door. She stood up, and the magazine fell to the floor. Her visitor turned out to be a lady collecting money for guide dogs. Her purse was on the hall table. This was a good cause, and the lady did have children who attended her school. She popped some money in the collection tin and returned to the lounge.

Somehow, the cheque had fallen off the table and landed on the magazine. *How had that happened?* she thought.

As she bent over to pick it up, she noticed it had fallen onto a page with a feature about a new development near to Carlisle. The development was named Conway Park – an exclusive complex of four-, five-, and six-bedroom properties on the edge of the city, tastefully built in a parkland setting.

Having returned her cheque to the table, she looked at the houses. They did look very well finished, but then she thought of the name. *Conway.* Had the cheque landed here on purpose to draw her attention to that name? The Conways featured in her story. Simon Newton was their nephew and cousin, and they had raised Simon when he lost his parents.

Gilly placed the magazine on the coffee table and sat back on the sofa. What was she to make of this? At first, she felt uneasy as before, but this was not unexpected. She was certain that there would be further developments in relation to her story and the characters involved. She sat for some while thinking things through.

If the Conways had lived locally, and Simon as well, someone around here would remember them. Yes, it was a long time ago – around eighteen years since she wrote her story – so these events may well have happened twenty-five or more years ago.

But who, and where, could she ask? Perhaps her father had known them. She would mention this tomorrow. If not, some of his friends and associates might. She remembered that the former Chief Constable of the county had been a good friend of his for many years.

Gilly began to feel more positive. She would turn detective. After all, the clues were there, and at least she was back in control. Then she remembered how her story had ended – completely blank. She had run out of ideas.

What if she wasn't meant to find out? Would it be unwise to do so? These doubts lingered, and she was sure they would remain unless she made efforts to unravel the clues. Gilly poured herself a gin and tonic to help her sleep. The drink did knock her out, and sleep well she did.

Friday morning came and, after a visit to the supermarket, she made a trip to the bank where she paid in her cheque. At first, she thought that just dropping in to see her father on the way home would suffice. However, if he had any information, the visit may take a little longer. She would see him after going home and having lunch.

After unpacking her shopping and having a snack, she decided to give her father a call to see if a visit would be convenient. Gilly rang him direct and was surprised by his reaction. For once he seemed pleased to hear from her, and he was looking forward to receiving a visit. She headed back to town, and on towards the home, in the countryside a little further away.

The home, Hardingsfield, was more like an exclusive

country hotel, accessed from a long drive through wood-land. The building was an extensive old manor house built from white brick. The large windows and doors allowed light to flood in.

Gilly parked on the right-hand side in front of her father's window. There was a wide flower bed between the drive and the wall, so from the car she couldn't see directly inside. He had insisted on a ground floor room, as the French doors to the side allowed him easy access to the grounds. It was to these doors she went, knowing they wouldn't be locked, and let herself in.

Her father sat in his expensive athlete's wheelchair. Charles Raymond had short, brown hair and a square face. He was strong-looking with a well-developed upper body from his use of the wheelchair.

"Good to see you, Gilly," he said, in remarkably good spirits.

"You seem very well, Daddy." Gilly approached her father, giving him a kiss.

"Your mother tells me you've had a trip to Carlisle. That was a long way to go," he said, giving her one of his looks.

She explained the reason for her trip and how well the McGregors had looked after her, and mentioned the generous payment she had received. She told him that she would be adding it to the fund for new equipment for the school. He was pleased she had been rewarded financially, and told her he would write a cheque for the same amount. She thanked him very much, although she wasn't too surprised. He had always been a generous father. Gilly gave him a hug and sat down. She enquired whether he was busy with his work.

"I can be as busy as I like these days. I have an excellent team in the office, so as long as I can keep my mind active, I'm fine," he replied.

"That sounds ideal, Daddy. It's good to know you're happy."

"Anyway, Gilly, haven't you and Jimmy got together yet?" He always asked this. It was if he was insisting they should be together.

"Jimmy and I are good friends, always have been and always will be, but I'm afraid we'll never be a couple," Gilly answered firmly.

"Sorry, Gilly. It's because I really like him. I'll try to remember your words in future," said Charles, looking over his glasses.

Gilly decided this would be a good time to enquire about the Conways.

"You have a good memory, Daddy. Can you remember a family by the name of Conway, who lived locally – around, say, twenty-five years ago?" she asked.

There was a brief silence.

"Conway," he said. "Can't say I do. Why do you ask?"

"Well, the McGregors who I visited in Carlisle might have known them. That's all," she said. "How about your friend who was Chief Constable? Perhaps he would recognise the name?"

"Oh, he won't remember anything. He has dementia and he's living in the south of France." Her father's tone had changed, so Gilly didn't pursue her questions any further.

"I'll be going for my swim soon," said Charles, looking at his watch.

"Do you swim every day?"

"Yes. The pool has been a real benefit for this place. You should have brought your costume!" His tone was more mellow now.

"Would that be allowed?" asked Gilly.

"Anything is allowed if you are the owner."

Gilly hadn't expected this. She knew her father was a wealthy man, but to own the home he was in, which had recently been given a major overhaul with the addition of the pool and sauna complex – that did come as a shock.

"I shall leave you to have your swim then," Gilly said.

She felt she had done her duty by visiting, and this time at least her father seemed happy. Usually when asked how he was, his answer was short and snappy: *I'm only half the man I was*.

"Thank you for visiting. I hope you'll call again soon,

and when you do, bring your swimming costume. You'll enjoy the new facilities."

It sounded as if Charles wanted to see his daughter more frequently, and if he could be pleasant like today, Gilly would be happy to make this happen. Charles moved his chair towards his desk.

"I'll write your cheque, Gilly," he said, as he pulled the top drawer open.

"That's very kind of you, Daddy. I'll have enough money soon to order the equipment."

Gilly held out her hand to receive the cheque, and placed it in her bag. She gave her father a kiss and promised to call again soon. She left through the French doors and walked around the corner to where she had parked at the front, and as she looked through his window, he was waving to her – something he had never done before. She waved back before driving away.

As she drove, she wondered at the change in her father's mood. He used to be this way on skiing holidays and other outings when she was growing up. Then, after his accident, he had become very depressed and moody. Today had been a breath of fresh air. She hadn't managed to extract any information regarding the Conways, but she did detect his change of tone when they were mentioned.

Gilly decided to visit her mother in the morning and mention her father's good mood. She wondered whether her mother had seen him like this, and whether she could explain the change.

Chapter 9

It was late on Saturday morning when Gilly arrived at her mother's house. When she stepped into the garden, her mother was attending to the washing on the line.

"I see you've been busy. I hope it doesn't rain," said Gilly.

"It's so bright and breezy, they shan't be out for long. Do you fancy a coffee?" her mother asked.

Gilly headed to the kitchen to make a drink, as her mother would be a little while before she was finished. They both sat down at the kitchen table to enjoy their coffee.

"I gave Daddy a visit yesterday afternoon," said Gilly, sipping her drink.

"Oh, you did? And how was he?"

"He was much happier than he's ever been since moving to Hardingfield. He was excellent company. Whatever happened to him?"

Julia smiled. "Did you go and see the pool and spa complex?"

"No, but he told me he swims daily. He invited me to join him on my next visit."

"Oh, did he?" Julia asked. "And has he mentioned the

new physiotherapist who attends to him while he's there?"

"He didn't mention a physio. A female physio, no doubt," said Gilly, and Julia nodded. "So that's why he's happy. I suppose she's attractive as well?"

"Your father finds her attractive," was Julia's reply.

"Don't you mind, Mummy? You never seem to be angry or jealous when there's another woman involved." Gilly had often wondered why they were still married. It was common knowledge he was a lady's man.

"We're still together, as such, because of his money. While there is a plentiful supply of that, he may do as he pleases. After all, anything below the waist is of no use to anyone any more. But if she can help him to swim and exercise, I'm all for it." Julia sounded quite definite on this.

"I wasn't aware he owned the nursing home. With the new complex being built, that must have been expensive," Gilly said, finishing her coffee.

"Oh, your father has extensive wealth. With the new facilities at the home, the fees for the other residents will no doubt increase. Your father is a very enterprising man."

Gilly stayed with her mother until after lunch. Before she left, Julia asked her daughter if there had been anymore revelations regarding the characters in her story. Gilly didn't mention the magazine feature about Conway Place, and how her cheque had landed directly on top of it. She knew her mother would call this another coincidence.

It was early afternoon when Gilly left for home, telling her mother she would catch up with her next week. When Gilly drove into her apartment car park, she noticed Jimmy Shaw's Land Rover parked in one of the other spaces. His company had converted the large, red-brick hall a few years earlier, so she assumed one of the residents wanted to make some changes. She locked her car and made her way home.

An hour passed before she heard a knock at the door, and she wasn't surprised to find Jimmy waiting outside. She invited him in. He was a large man, around six-foot-four, very thick-set. He'd made an ideal rugby player, and he still played occasionally. His nose had been broken during a game, and with his short-cropped, light brown hair, this made him look quite intimidating. No one would argue with Jimmy Shaw. But despite his appearance, he was a lovely person, and Gilly liked him very much.

"It's good to see you, Jimmy. Are you here to check on a job?"

He nodded. "The Roberts want to change their kitchen, so I came to talk through some ideas with them."

"Oh, that doesn't surprise me. Mrs Roberts changes things in her home more frequently than she changes her underwear," said Gilly, with a large grin on her face.

They sat down in the lounge, and Gilly told him about her trip to Carlisle and meeting the McGregors, and how she had returned better off. She also mentioned her father's good mood. Gilly knew it was Jimmy's company who had built the pool and spa complex, and she wanted to try and find out how much he had spent.

She made several attempts to ask in a roundabout way, but Jimmy, who was usually very direct, would not divulge any information. He would only say that there had been several alterations to the plans as the work progressed, and that the final costs were still to be established.

Jimmy stayed for a drink, and talked about the plans for the new primary school. His company had won the contract for the building, which pleased Gilly. Jimmy's father and uncle had run an established business for many years, and always prided themselves on providing quality, first-class work. As a partner in the business, Jimmy would one day take over completely. She suspected that her father's wish for Jimmy and Gilly to get together had more to do with financial security than her happiness. Both men were driven by making money, a view she certainly didn't share.

The daylight was disappearing when Jimmy left. It had been good to see him. They did get on well, but Jimmy was always at work. When the time came to take over the business completely, she knew the job would control his life.

Chapter 10

Gilly planned a relaxing evening after preparing for school on Monday, where she realised she might be able to find some more information about the Conways.

She was pleased to return to school. In some ways this was her life, including running after-school sessions such as swimming and arts-and-crafts events. Gilly's donation, from the McGregors and from her father, was gratefully received by the headmistress, who revealed she could now place the order for the gym equipment they needed.

Headmistress Angela Summers was in her late fifties, a very tall and slender lady. She had long brown hair, which she kept coloured. She looked much younger than she was, with unblemished skin and a very pretty face. Through the years Gilly had known her, she had never been annoyed or angry in any way, an example Gilly had always tried to follow. Angela was a good friend to all her teachers, and Gilly liked her very much. So, when the opportunity arose, she asked Angela about the Conways.

"It's a fairly common name, so I should remember." Angela ran her fingers along the chain of her necklace. "I can't recall any child by that name in any of my classes. I'll have to think back to the late sixties, maybe early seventies.

It was a long time ago."

Gilly knew she would do her best to remember, and when Angela asked about the reason for her interest, once again she justified it by saying that the McGregors may have met the Conways years ago.

The McGregors were still in her thoughts, and had promised to stay in touch, but she would leave it for a few weeks so there would be plenty to talk about.

The weeks passed quickly, and Gilly was kept busy at school. This was her life, and she loved it. Before she knew it, Easter was fast approaching. The weather was very good for the time of year, and she hoped the sunny and fine conditions would last over the Easter break.

Just before the term ended, the local vicar visited to give his Easter sermon to the whole school. Reverend Miles was elderly, and usually mumbled his way through his services. Although the children were asked to pay attention, they usually ended up chatting amongst themselves.

The last day of term came, and the teachers and all the pupils congregated in the hall after lunch for the Easter sermon. Gilly had noticed a different car in the school car park. It caught her attention, as her father's close friend and car dealer, Geoffrey Payne, used to own one. It was a vintage Jenson Interceptor in a lovely gold colour.

The Reverend seemed to be taking his time coming into the hall, and the children were talking, although not noisily. As their voices grew steadily louder, without any warning, there was an almighty clap from the back of the hall. Everyone's heads turned, to see a different minister with the headmistress walking towards the front of the room.

"Now, everyone. I'd like you to meet Reverend Jacobs, who has kindly stepped in as dear old Reverend Miles is unwell. So, over to you, Linden."

Angela walked to the side of the hall, and Reverend Jacobs took his place in front of the children.

He was a large, tall man, who reminded Gilly of a James Bond figure. He looked so serious as his eyes scanned the children before him. He had a squarish face and distinct features.

"Who would like to listen to the story of Easter told by a crusty old vicar?"

His voice was deep and rather menacing. He looked at the children as very few hands went into the air.

"Hmm." He responded. "Well. Who would like to act out the story of Easter in the form of a play?"

His tone was much softer, and after he had spoken there was a definite smile on his face. Everyone's hand was raised and the hall was filled with excitement.

Considering he had never met the children before, his casting was excellent, with some of Gilly's class included. The children sat around the edge of the hall as the Reverend conducted the drama group. He had an excellent way with them, guiding and pointing them in the right directions. It certainly was entertaining, and everyone was treated to a lively and enjoyable performance. At the end, the applause was deafening, with the Reverend standing back and clapping for the performers. This would certainly be an Easter to remember.

Miss Summers stepped in to say a huge 'thank you' to Reverend Jacobs, and once again there was huge applause. Gilly and one of her fellow teachers took the children out into the playground to let off even more steam. Angela and the other teachers remained in the hall, talking to Reverend Jacobs about how he had transformed the mood in the school during his short visit. A while later, Angela appeared at the school door and beckoned Gilly to return inside. Gilly found her talking to the Reverend, and on approaching, she was introduced. "Now, Linden, I would like you to meet Miss Raymond. I am hoping that when I retire, she will be selected to take over my position, and then to be head of the new school when it opens," said Angela, optimistically.

"I hope you realise Angela will be a very hard act to follow, Miss Raymond," said Linden with a firm handshake.

"Well, Reverend, I have yet to be selected! If I am, it will be a huge honour, and a challenge I'll look forward to immensely."

Linden nodded approvingly. "Then your selection will be certain, I'm sure."

"Thank you, Reverend. However, the other candidates are also committed, and we will have to see," replied Gilly.

"The position is yours, of that I am sure."

The expression on his face and those exact words he had used took her back to the time she had met Simon Newton. *Of that, I am sure*, Simon had said, when she mentioned seeing him again. Somehow, these things felt connected, but instead of asking why he thought it was certain the job would be hers, she simply said, "Thank you, Reverend. You are very kind."

"Oh, my goodness, look at the time. The children will be leaving soon."

Angela's comment had everyone looking at their watches, and soon afterwards the children returned to their classrooms to collect their books for the Easter break.

The bell rang and the excited children made their way out of school and into the playground. Gilly could see Angela near the Reverend's sports car, and before anyone else could leave there was a beefy roar from the car's engine. Linden waved to the children as he drove away, and his car could be heard disappearing into the distance. The children, who should have been gone by now, were all waving and chanting, 'Linden, Linden,' until he was well out of sight.

When the teachers met with Angela, they all agreed what a successful afternoon it had been, and asked whether Reverend Jacobs could return – perhaps at Christmas. Angela revealed that she had known him for some time, but because it was Reverend Miles's parish, she couldn't risk offending him by favouring Reverend Jacobs. Gilly commented, pointing out what a difference Linden had made, and suggesting the two men could work together, or run alternate sermons, as a sort of compromise. Angela said she hoped to sort something out, as she knew how successful the afternoon had been.

During the Easter break, Gilly received a visit from her mother, who came over unexpectedly one afternoon. Gilly mentioned Reverend Jacobs, and how he had transformed the school in the short time he was there.

"I've worked for people who needed my floristry services at his church, so I know exactly what you mean," said Julia. "He's what you might call a maverick priest – not to everyone's taste, but we got on really well."

Gilly told her mother about his comments regarding her taking over as headmistress, and the words and expressions he had used, identical to Simon Newton.

"I think you'll find that Reverend Jacobs knows a great deal," commented Julia.

"Will you see him in the near future?" asked Gilly. Her mother wasn't sure, but added that she could arrange to.

"Without making it obvious, would you ask him if he has ever known a Simon Newton? And how he can be so sure about my appointment as Headmistress?" Gilly asked.

Her mother sighed. "I know it will be difficult to extract information from him. He's a master of secrecy, so I shall have to approach this in a roundabout way. I can't make any promises. Anyway – haven't you moved on from this Simon Newton thing?"

"I am in control of the situation, but I want to find out why these strange things are happening," Gilly replied.

During the Easter holidays, Gilly decided to catch up with the McGregors. She rang their number one evening with no success – only a message that this number was no longer available. She made several attempts, but the message was always the same. Gilly concluded that they must have changed their number, for whatever reason, and that they would either ring her or write to inform her of the change.

The school holiday soon passed. The next term was underway, and after a few weeks Gilly had still heard nothing from the McGregors. She decided to write and ask if all was well, and to tell them that the school would soon have its much-needed gym equipment, thanks to their generous payment. Gilly was certain that after a couple of weeks or so, there would either be a call or a reply.

After a week and a half Gilly returned home from

school late on a Thursday afternoon, and found amongst her mail an envelope with a Carlisle postmark on. The writing didn't look familiar, but then she had only noticed Audrey's writing in her magazines, where Audrey had already completed the crosswords.

Gilly decided to read her correspondence after tea, so after eating and bathing she settled down on her sofa with a drink, put her feet up, and started opening her post. She saved the McGregor's letter until last, but when she opened the envelope and looked at the letter, she realised it wasn't from the McGregors at all. The letter had been sent by the Masons from the large house opposite the McGregors.

Dear Miss Raymond, it began.

Chapter 11

Dear Miss Raymond,

    I am taking delivery of the McGregor's post, and felt I needed to reply to your letter. The McGregors spoke of your visit, and during the short time they knew you, they came to like you very much. I do hope, Miss Raymond, that you are sitting down, as I am afraid you will find the contents of my letter somewhat disturbing.

    Just before Easter, my husband Peter and I retired for the evening at around ten o'clock, as we usually do. Both of us are light sleepers and usually wake up a couple of times during the night. On that particular evening, we were woken around midnight by a light that was lighting up our bedroom. It was Peter who went to investigate, and he was shocked when he looked out between the curtains to find that the McGregors' house was on fire.

    I rang 999 for the fire brigade, and we quickly pulled on some clothes and headed downstairs. We made our way into the road to find out if we could help. We were hoping to see the McGregors and offer support and accommodation for as long as needed. We saw no one, but we could hear sirens in the distance. The downstairs windows had shattered, and the flames were pouring out.

The fire was intense. We looked upstairs and we could see figures at the window desperately trying to get out. It was horrific to see and, both of us being elderly, we could only pray the fire engine would arrive soon.

As the engine approached there was a large blast, as the windows smashed and the flames poured out. We realised there could be no survivors. Three fire crews attended and remained for several hours to bring the blaze under control. We had been unable to do anything, and I'm ashamed to say that when we noticed the figures at the window, we both looked away and cried. We felt absolutely helpless.

Investigations into the cause of the fire revealed two bodies, and these could only be identified using dental records. It has been confirmed that the bodies were Doctor and Mrs McGregor. The investigations into the cause of the fire proved inconclusive, but it seems that the fire was not suspicious.

During the team's investigations, they discovered something very strange. Beneath the debris and rubble, they found one of Doctor McGregor's dolls. She had survived the fire without any damage at all, which seems impossible to believe, as she was made of china. Her hair and clothes were intact. It seemed as if someone had taken her away, and after the fire had returned her, placing rubble over her.

I can't believe this either. Who would do such a thing? And Doctor McGregor would never allow anyone to take a doll. I did see the doll before it was removed. When I last spoke to Doctor McGregor he told me he had added a prize doll to his collection, and fitted the original hand, which you had kindly brought for him. From the description of the doll, I am certain she is the survivor – all very strange to me.

The remains of the house are unsafe and due for demolition. There are metal barriers all around and we both find it disturbing to see. We feel that after what has happened, we can no longer stay here, and we are looking for a much smaller property, perhaps in a different location. If anything else transpires I will let you know, but for now, I am deeply sorry to be the bearer of such horrific and dreadful news.

Yours, Caroline Mason.

Gilly placed the letter on the table. How could this have happened? She had only known the McGregors for a short while. They were very kind and caring people who had lost their lives in the most horrific way, and yet the doll had survived – along with the hand.

Would this have happened if she hadn't found the hand? Gilly felt convinced that this had been partly her fault. Before, it had been strange that what she had written had seemed to come true, but she had never imagined any loss of life, especially not for people she really liked. This was becoming too much.

Her mother's efforts to explain things had convinced her not to be concerned by these events, and to accept that not everything in life could be explained. But for there to be deaths, for which she felt partly responsible, and with the doll's mysterious survival – how could she cope with this?

She tried to pick up her drink, only to return the glass to table as her hand was shaking so much. She thought about what might happen next. She couldn't call her mother. Not today. She was in too much of a state. And what about tomorrow? How could she go to school and teach?

The evening passed very slowly. Gilly was unable to focus on anything except the contents of the letter, which kept going through her mind. It was the same when she should have been sleeping, and by the morning she hadn't slept at all.

Gilly got out of bed at her usual time. She felt ghastly and unable to focus on anything. She would have to ring in and make an excuse for today. At least that would give her the weekend to gather her thoughts. Gilly made the call to the school, and spoke to Angela. Apparently, there was a bug going around, and Angela mentioned it before Gilly could fabricate some ailment of her own. Angela assumed Gilly was another victim of the illness, advised her to rest, and hoped to see her next week. *At least that part was easily sorted*, Gilly thought with relief as she put the phone down.

She managed to make herself some toast and a large

mug of black coffee. Perhaps with this, and the thought of a refreshing shower, she could get through the day. After her shower, she put on clean pyjamas and returned to her comfortable sofa.

It was then that she slept, not waking until around half-past five in the afternoon. Gilly was pleased to have slept for so long, and relieved that she felt hungry. She put a quick meal together and afterwards watched some television. Physically she was feeling better, but the thought of recent events weighed heavily on her mind. She thought about calling her mother, but decided to give the situation considerable thought by herself, rather than letting her mother pick up the pieces.

She turned the television off, and once again read through the letter. Mrs Mason had said that investigations had been carried out, and had ruled out suspicious circumstances, but how would they be sure with a fire so intense and destructive? Gilly tried to come up with some theories as to what had happened. She had not known the McGregors for very long, but they were people she really liked. They did have some strange ways, though. Most of all, treating the doll collection as their children. And what of the herbal tea Ian had made using marijuana?

This felt like an important lead. Doctor McGregor had been a quiet man, and very gentle. He and Audrey, who was so dominant, had suited each other well.

Could he be cultivating marijuana? she wondered.

Yes, he could – for the purpose of using it for herbal tea. So how about selling it to users to make money? That didn't seem like Ian at all. Then again, she had only spent a short while with them both, so really anything was possible. Perhaps he was selling drugs to addicts at a price which was affordable, which certainly wouldn't be ideal – but it might stop them stealing from others.

Had he been discovered by serious drug dealers? Had they stopped him once and for all? The more she thought about it, the more likely this seemed, but she had no evidence. If only she had visited his greenhouses and seen some plants growing! But he had been keen for her not to visit that part of the garden, and perhaps it would have been too early in the year for a crop. Maybe it was Audrey who was behind this – or were they in it together?

All she had was speculation.

Gilly thought about sending Mrs Mason a reply to see if there had been any developments, but she was elderly and had really been disturbed by the tragedy, so that wouldn't be fair. All these theories were plausible, but none of them explained why the doll had survived, which was a mystery itself. Someone must have taken her, and returned her to the house when the rubble had cooled down. Gilly couldn't think of any explanation for this.

The evening passed quickly. Having slept through the

day, Gilly wondered what sort of night she would have. After thinking things through, she felt she was no longer totally responsible for the tragic events – but there was something odd about Bedina's survival.

The McGregors' lives had been destroyed, as had Simon Newton's, along with the Conway family. She had been inspired to write about the Conways when she had found the doll's hand, and then discovered that what she had written had been true.

Were they all connected by the doll? If so, what would be her fate for being the custodian of the hand, and for reuniting it with Bedina? Could she expect a car accident, or a fire? Must she live her life in fear?

No – she wasn't going to let that happen. Gilly enjoyed her life, and her job at the school. She was excited about the possibility of taking over as head when the new school was built, so she had a great deal to look forward to. She was determined that recent events would not change things for her.

She slept well, and rose at about half-past eight. Over breakfast, she wondered how to use her day. If she was to go shopping, someone from the school would be sure to see her – and yesterday she had claimed to have the bug that was apparently going around. She decided it would be best to stay at home. She planned to return to school on Monday, so she would spend the day planning for the coming week.

On Sunday, Gilly received a phone call from her mother. They chatted for around half an hour. Gilly decided not to mention the letter she had received – not yet, anyway – but her mother could tell that something wasn't right. She knew her daughter too well, but she left it up to Gilly to say if there was something wrong, in her own time.

Gilly did return to school the following week. She tried very hard to forget the contents of Mrs Mason's letter, and to try and get on with her life as best as she could. Later that week, two of her brightest girls stayed behind one lunchtime and remained sitting at their desks. Gilly asked why they hadn't joined their friends to have lunch and play. Their reply was, "We are worried about you, Miss Raymond. You seem so different this week."

Gilly gave them an encouraging smile. "I'm fine, girls, really. I've had some upsetting news, that's all. I'll soon be back to my old self, and I really appreciate your concern. Now, please go and have your lunch."

She realised she needed to find a way to lift her spirits, if only for the time she was at school.

Chapter 12

The next person to notice was Jimmy Shaw, who asked if he could take her to the local Steam and Country Fair. Gilly promised to let him know. It was kind of him to invite her, and this might be just what she needed, instead of thinking about what had happened.

When Gilly visited her mother the next weekend, she took the letter. She was interested to see her reaction. Julia was pleased to hear her daughter had accepted Jimmy's offer to take her to the show. Recently she had felt that her daughter had become reclusive and, apart from her work, not interested in much at all.

Over coffee in her mother's kitchen, Gilly produced Mrs Mason's letter. Julia put on her reading glasses and read carefully.

"Oh, dear, how dreadful! Those poor people. I can see why you've seemed down in the dumps recently."

Gilly was relieved by her mother's reaction, and asked for her thoughts. What had happened? Why had the doll survived?

"Well, darling. This is very strange, all of it. The McGregors were good people, according to you, and you are a very good judge of character – that I know. The fire does seem suspicious, especially for them to be trapped like that. If your theory about Ian producing drugs proves to be correct, I'm sure the police will investigate. Hopefully they'll find whoever is responsible, and put them away for a very long time.

"Now, the doll? That's another matter, and my thoughts are these. The doll was away for expert repair, or to be valued – we'll never know the reason, but she wasn't in the house for the fire. The person looking after her must have returned her, and placed her where she was found."

Gilly looked bemused at her mother's explanations.

"Why?" she asked.

"When there's a tragedy or a house fire reported on the news you always see endless teddy bears left outside the houses. Ian's doll is no different. That's how I see it."

Gilly realised her mother could well be right, and for now she needed something logical to believe in.

By believing her mother, and her own drugs theory, she no longer felt responsible for the fire. She could only wish that she had never found the hand. At least then, she wouldn't have known about any of this.

Gilly's time at school was more enjoyable now. Better weather had arrived, and she loved to take her class outdoors so they could learn about the natural world. It seemed to inspire them so much. The date of the Aldbridge Country Fair was fast approaching.

Gilly had accepted Jimmy's offer to go. It was something she was looking forward to, and she hoped the good weather would continue.

Jimmy arranged to pick Gilly up on the morning of the show. He had promised to give his Land Rover a good clean and dress himself in something presentable. Gilly could only remember seeing him in working gear, so when she heard a knock at the door she was pleasantly surprised to see him looking so smart. He was wearing a well-ironed beige shirt with short sleeves, mid-brown corduroy trousers, and a very smart tweed waistcoat. Even his shoes, a pair of tan brogues, looked brand new.

"Good heavens, Jimmy, you do look smart! You'll certainly catch people's eyes today," Gilly said.

"Well, you look pretty good yourself," he replied, as they walked to the Land Rover.

Gilly could see it was clean – very clean. Jimmy opened the door for Gilly. Inside was gleaming as well, a bit different to the builder's van she remembered, filled with endless drinks cans, food wrappings, and general rubbish.

"We had it valeted especially for the occasion," Jimmy explained. "It's even surprised me how good it looks!"

If Gilly had known this, she could have worn something different. However, her denim jeans were new, and at least her white blouse – one of her favourites – wouldn't be marked by dirty seats. She wore an orange silk scarf and brown knee-high boots.

The Aldbridge Country Fair was held on farmland, about half an hour's drive away from Gilly's home. Over the years it had grown to become an important date in the country calendar. The day was sunny and warm for late spring, and when they arrived many people were there already.

Gilly was determined to enjoy her day. After all, it had begun well with Jimmy's appearance and a clean vehicle. *What could possibly go wrong?*

Jimmy was keen to see the steam engines. He suggested that they look around them first and speak to the owners. Then they would then move on to the trade tents and the events taking place in the show ring. To his surprise, Gilly was really interested in the engines, and asked the owners all sorts of questions.

"I had no idea you would find these so interesting, Gilly," Jimmy said.

Gilly laughed. "The children in my class will love all these stories! I'm planning to use the photos in the programme to help them explore our rural heritage. I'm sure plenty of children from school will be here, and next week everything they've seen will be fresh in their minds. It's a great opportunity."

After a hot dog and a drink from the bar, the pair made their way to the trade tents, where Gilly commented that she hoped Jimmy would have as much interest in the crafts and items for sale. They did spend a while talking with the traders, and once again Gilly showed considerable interest in the craft items, and the people who had made them. Eventually they made their way to the show ring and found a vacant straw bale to sit on. They were treated to a show of livestock, followed by dog agility, and a dog show. All the events were entertaining and the afternoon flew by.

Gilly had been pleased to see children from school, and from her class, at the fair taking an interest.

"Thank you, Jimmy," she said. "This has been a really enjoyable day – something I really needed."

Jimmy put his arm around her and she rested her head on his shoulder. She had seen Jimmy differently today. He had made a tremendous effort with his appearance and a clean vehicle, and he had been an absolute pleasure to be with. She found she was looking forward to the next time they could spend time together – as surely there would be a next time.

She briefly closed her eyes, and when she opened them, she had a clear view across the show ring. The dogs had left, and the next event was to be a parade of vintage tractors. It was then that she noticed a man sitting down on the opposite side. He had grey hair and a beard, and was wearing glasses. He was some distance away, but he did bear a remarkable likeness to Ian McGregor. She closed her eyes for a moment, thinking she had been mistaken, but when she opened them, he was still there.

"Jimmy, can you see that man on the other side? Grey hair, beard, glasses – sitting nearly opposite us?" Gilly asked.

Jimmy looked across the show ring. "Yes. Why? Do you know him?"

"He looks identical to Ian McGregor, who I went to see in Carlisle," she replied.

"Well, perhaps it is, Gilly. Shall we go and see?"

Gilly felt a familiar sense of hesitation.

Should she, or shouldn't she?

"Yes. In a moment," she said, shaking her head. "But it's not him. He's dead."

"I'm so sorry." Jimmy spoke gently. "I didn't know."

Gilly stood up, her eyes still focused on the man. Jimmy stood, and the pair walked around the perimeter of the ring, Gilly's eyes firmly fixed on Ian's lookalike. The next thing she knew, two guys walked across in front of them and blocked her view. Jimmy walked around them, followed by Gilly, and as she looked to where the man was sitting, she realised he had disappeared.

Gilly stopped, and Jimmy turned back to her.

"Oh, he's gone," she said, sounding lost. "We need to find him. He can't have gone far." She made her way between the tents outside the show ring, and Jimmy followed.

They both spent some while looking and thinking about where he might have gone, but he had indeed disappeared. When they returned to the ring, the place where he was sitting had been taken by another man. Jimmy made his way through the crowd to ask the people either side of where he had been sitting whether they knew who he was, but no one did. Eventually, the two of them returned to some spare places on the straw bales, ready for the parade of vintage tractors. Jimmy was looking forward to the parade, but Gilly, who had been enjoying the day immensely, now felt deflated. All she wanted to do was go home. She thought it would be unreasonable to ask Jimmy to leave early, so she decided to stay until he was ready to go, but Jimmy noticed the change in her behaviour. After the tractors had made their way into the ring, Jimmy asked if she would like to leave.

"Well, I would," she admitted, "but I know you'll want to talk to the owners after the parade. I don't want to spoil your day."

"Let me take you home, Gilly. I don't want to keep you here if you'd rather go."

Gilly was surprised by Jimmy's reaction. She re-alised that he really cared for her, something she hadn't experienced for a long time, and she was very grateful to have such a good friend.

It was Jimmy who spoke most on the journey home. He

knew she had been upset by seeing this man who resembled her friend. He, too, had enjoyed the day, and he realised a sensitive approach was necessary.

After arriving home, Gilly made coffee while Jimmy sat in the lounge. Gilly found the letter from Mrs Mason and asked Jimmy to read it.

"How horrific," he said, with genuine sympathy. "I can see this has affected you deeply – and seeing Ian's lookalike this afternoon won't have helped at all."

Jimmy placed the letter on the table and took a sip of his coffee.

"You did see the man I saw, didn't you, Jimmy?"

Jimmy nodded. "Oh, yes. I saw him. He was real."

There was a long silence before Jimmy asked, "How well did you know the McGregors, then?"

"Only briefly, I suppose, but they were the sort of people you felt at home with straight away. As if you'd known them forever, if you can understand that."

Jimmy nodded. "Did he mention whether he had a brother?"

"No, why would he?" asked Gilly.

"Well, say he did. Perhaps they were twins, and that's who we saw today."

Jimmy's theory seemed far too convenient for Gilly. "I think he would have mentioned that," she said.

"Perhaps he didn't know. Maybe they were separated at

birth, and maybe neither of them knew they had a sibling. Surely that's a possibility."

Gilly thought for a while. "That's all speculation, though. Possible, yes, but likely? I don't know."

"Isn't that life, though?" Jimmy asked. "All about beliefs, and what you choose to believe? Making things make sense so you can move on?"

Jimmy was giving her ideas to think about. Perhaps he was right, and she should believe a version of this story they had pieced together. But she knew she would have to rethink her theory the next time something happened – and she was sure there would be a next time.

Chapter 13

The following week, her spirits were lifted by her class, who had taken an interest in her account of the Country Fair, including several children who had attended themselves. Gilly was a great believer that if children could experience the subjects she taught, they would show a great deal of interest. On previous occasions she had arranged farm visits, and she, along with other teachers, had created a school garden, which had proved a great success. When construction on the new school began, she had insisted that all of the children should visit the site during the various stages of construction, and Jimmy had been more than happy to oblige.

A few weeks passed, and school life was good. Jimmy had called to see her on a few occasions, but the local demand for construction had picked up, and work was taking up most of his time. Gilly, who had always been able to enjoy a good night's rest, had started to wake at around two or three o'clock, and was unable to sleep afterwards. Although this wasn't happening every night, when it did occur she would feel very drained as the afternoon arrived.

Gilly's disturbed nights continued, once or twice a week. On these occasions, she would get up and sit in the lounge and read, usually with a large glass of gin or two. However, she knew this was unwise. Driving to school and then teaching under the influence of drink would be totally irresponsible. She decided that a much better option would be to pick up some sleeping pills from the pharmacy. These were successful at first, and she managed to enjoy several good nights of rest. At last, she felt she had found some stability in her life.

After about two weeks, Gilly started to dream she was walking somewhere, through some residential area, and the sky was red like a huge beacon. She would then wake when she needed to get up. The dreams continued, perhaps twice a week. Each time she found herself a little further along the same street, and the sky became even brighter.

Could this be some effect of the sleeping pills? They knocked her out, and with that she was feeling much better. Her dreams continued, and one night she realised what they were about. In her dream, a little further along the same street, she crossed the road. The sky was even brighter. The sign on the corner of the street read 'Victoria Place'.

Gilly was in Carlisle, in the road leading to the McGregors' house. The sky was red because of the fire, and she was heading towards it. As before, she woke up in time for school, but felt very disturbed. She wondered where her dreams were heading, and why she was having these dreams at all. Perhaps she should take a break from her medication and see what would happen. She decided that the weekend would be a suitable time try this, and see what effect it might have.

The dreams she was having continued. She walked along Victoria Place towards the McGregors', finally reaching the burning house. There was a small crowd of people gathered in the street. Gilly wanted to walk past, but instead she turned towards the inferno and focused on the upstairs windows. She could hear fire engine sirens, and people saying they would be too late to save lives.

It was then she realised she could see figures at the window, as Mrs Mason had described. It was an awful and horrific sight, followed by the windows shattering and fierce flames pouring out of the openings.

Gilly woke at her usual time. It was Saturday morning, and the dream left her even more disturbed and shaken. She didn't have to go out today, and felt she couldn't anyway. Over breakfast, she wondered what this was all about. Perhaps these dreams would stop, now that she had reached the house and witnessed the fire.

She knew from Mrs Mason's letter how disturbing the events had been. Once again, she decided to pick herself up and move on until the next unnerving event, whenever and whatever this might be. Since her disturbed nights and her recurring nightmares, Gilly had become reclusive – not even visiting her mother, going out with friends, or seeing her father. She decided that this would have to change. She was determined to resume a normal life, but for the rest of the weekend she would relax and unwind.

Gilly returned to school on Monday morning. She had decided to focus on her work and devote all her attention to her class. She thought it was time all of the children had a visit to the new school site, but before she could arrange this with Jimmy, she would need approval from the head-mistress. After the children had gone home, and most of the teachers had left, she made her way to Angela's office. Angela was pleased see her, and welcomed Gilly in.

"Please sit down. Would you care for a drink?" asked Angela.

Gilly declined. She revealed her proposals for the site visit, while Angela listened without saying a word. Gilly knew that this was Angela's way, and that she would only give her verdict at the end. Her say would be final, and Gilly had never known her to be wrong.

"I think this is just what the children need, Gilly. Please do speak to Jimmy! Ask for some flexibility with the arrangements, and I will talk to the coach company to discuss transport." Angela was fully behind her idea, which meant so much to Gilly.

"Now you're here, Gilly, how are you feeling at the moment?" Angela asked.

Gilly knew telling her she was fine wouldn't convince her.

"I wonder why you ask," she replied.

"I've heard that you haven't been yourself for a while. Is there something you'd like to discuss with me?"

Gilly realised she should tell Angela about her lack of sleep, and about the dreams she'd been having. She started to explain, mentioning the sleeping pills, and ending with the awful dream about the McGregors.

Once more Angela listened, only speaking when Gilly had finished.

"It would appear that the doll was cursed," she said.

"Do you believe in that sort of thing?" asked Gilly.

Angels shook her head. "We'll never know for sure, but since you travelled to Carlisle you've seemed somewhat removed at times."

Oh dear, Gilly thought. She was hoping to become the new head in around eighteen months, and she'd need to prove herself if she wanted the job.

"I'm more focused than ever, Angela," she responded, "and that's how I mean to continue from now on."

"That's what I like to hear," Angela nodded. "Any further problems, and you come to me straight away."

"Thank you very much. Will this affect my chances of taking over when you retire?" Gilly asked, nervously.

Angela gave a broad smile and shook her head. "Not at all," she said.

Two things had occurred to Gilly following her meeting

with Angela. One – it seemed that Angela knew more about her experiences since finding the doll's hand than she had expected. Gilly wondered how could she could have found out. The only person Gilly had told was her mother and, seeing as her mother didn't care much for Angela, they were hardly likely to have discussed her feelings.

Gilly had often asked why her mother didn't like Angela. However, Julia had refused to talk about her, giving no explanation and being sharp with her daughter. Gilly knew not to pursue this matter further.

The second thing she took from her meeting was that the job of headmistress would be hers, following Angela's retirement. Gilly had expected a lecture, and to be told that she must do much better if she was to become the new head. After all, other teachers had expressed interest when Angela announced that she planned to retire, but Gilly was favoured because she had once taken over when Angela was ill, and everyone had been impressed with her work during her time in charge.

Now was the time to get a grip, and concentrate on her school work. Gilly planned to call Jimmy to arrange the site visits. With all that had gone on, they hadn't spoken for a while, and Jimmy had been very busy. The school project was only one of the sites the company had taken on. Rather than managing one project, he seemed to spend his days visiting other sites across the county, and was not always easy to contact.

She eventually made contact with Jimmy, and arranged the site visits. The builders were making good progress, and Jimmy was keen to show the children the new school plans. During their visit, he explained the processes and stages of construction. He made it all seem very interesting, and the children engaged well with him and with his workforce. All the site visits were entertaining, and proved very popular with the children.

Once more, Gilly could see that Jimmy was a very kind and caring man, and everyone had great respect for him. The school building wouldn't be completed until well into the following year. Gilly requested another visit at a later stage in the build, and everyone seemed happy to oblige.

With the summer holidays fast approaching, Gilly decided not to go away on the usual school trip with the other teachers and some of the children, as she had always done before. It was a decision she found hard to make, as in previous years these trips had been very enjoyable. This year was different, and if something were to disrupt her, she felt she would be unable to remain positive and calm.

Gilly spent her holiday preparing for the next school year, and helping her mother with a clear-out at her old farmhouse. She was still keen to move somewhere smaller, so a gradual clearing-out process seemed a good idea.

Julia had lived alone in the house for many years, and

it seemed such a waste of a large property. In the past, she had kept two Labradors for company, and to take on long walks. They had both died about two years ago, and Julia missed them dreadfully. However, she had plans to downsize and go away for some extended breaks, so she decided it would be unfair to take on more dogs and then place them in kennels for weeks on end.

When they were clearing things out, Gilly came across a photo of herself with her pet spaniel, Lola.

"Wasn't she a lovely dog, and a dear friend to have back then?" remarked Gilly.

Julia took the photo. "Yes," she replied. "And she was a very intelligent dog, from what I can remember."

Gilly thought for a moment. Her mother was right. She remembered how Lola, who had always slept in her room, right from when she was a puppy, had had a spell one summer when she wouldn't come into her bedroom at all. She had mostly stayed downstairs in the kitchen. At the time this had seemed odd, and they had assumed it was cooler downstairs, but now things were coming back to her.

It was the same summer when she had discovered the doll's hand, and put it in her desk drawer. Lola must have known there was something about the hand – she had been avoiding it. Perhaps Gilly should have sensed this and returned it to the chest in the barn, but back then everything in life had seemed like an adventure.

"You look deep in thought, darling," said Julia.

"I'm thinking about Lola, and how she kept away from my bedroom when I had taken the doll's hand and put in my drawer."

Julia smiled. "Oh, yes. Dogs can sense if something is wrong. After all, she certainly didn't like your father."

Gilly realised her mother was right. Lola had taken no notice of him at all, that she could remember.

Chapter 14

The long holiday seemed never-ending, which was nice. Usually it was broken up by the school excursion, and seemed to fly by far too quickly. Gilly was pleased to be helping her mother. The weather was unusually fair this year, and they would often head to the beach.

What had surprised Gilly was how well she was getting on with her father. He was cheerful, and never down as he had been in the past. He seemed to have discovered a real zest for life. This was definitely because of the new physio at his home.

When Gilly went to visit, she would use the pool and sauna, which was an absolute luxury. Her father would join her with Inge, the young and very attractive physio. She was German, and her English was perfect, as was her petite body. She was also a delightful person to be with, and Gilly liked her very much.

In many ways, life was good. Her parents, although apart, were happy – very happy, and at times like these, so was she. But there were always the recent events, which could not be erased, and Gilly couldn't help feeling that there would be more.

She concentrated on living one day at a time. Gilly was

keen to see more of Jimmy, and she had the feeling he felt the same. However, the construction business was growing fast, and taking on more and more developments. Jimmy spent most of his time supervising the jobs and finding tradesmen – good tradesmen he could trust to carry out work to the high standards the company required.

The holiday passed, and Gilly was pleased to return to school. It was an exciting time, with so many new faces. Gilly went out of her way to make them all feel at ease. The first few weeks seemed to pass instantly, and soon it was time for the annual school visit to Brook Marsh.

Brook Marsh was a nature reserve, some twenty or so miles away. The owners of an old quarry had done a tremendous job of planting several thousand trees, and creating lagoons and islands linked by boardwalks. Two years ago, a new visitor centre had opened. Schools were welcome to visit, and booking ahead was essential. The staff and volunteers were all knowledgeable about the reserve, and very kind to the children, even if sometimes they didn't deserve it.

The weather in late September was excellent. The mornings were cool and the days warm and sunny – ideal conditions for the visit. The coaches that had brought the children to school remained, ready for the trip. After assembly, they returned to the coaches with their bags of packed lunches, and Gilly brought several pairs of binoculars she had purchased since their last visit. Today would be a good day. Everything was going well.

Gilly sat next to Allan. She liked Allan – he was always kind and always calm. Nothing could fluster him. He wasn't a tall man or well-built, and he could never intimidate the children, but he was a very clever man. In some ways, he would make an excellent headteacher, but that role seemed destined for Gilly.

The reserve's entrance was off a main road, and easily accessible, so both Gilly and Allan were surprised when the driver made a left-hand turn, and drove through the village of Westbrook. The village was pretty, and opened up onto a large green. This proved to be a problem for the coach, which slowed and stopped at the edge of the grass. Ahead was a large bin lorry, blocking the road and leaving no space for the coach to pass.

"So much for the short cut," said Allan in a quiet voice.

"Indeed!" replied Gilly.

Gilly, who up until now had been reading, looked up at the green and the houses dotted around. The nearest house was large. It was modern in style, unlike the neighbouring houses, although there were small signs of wear and tear that marked it out as being a few decades old.

"I'm guessing there were several objections before that house was built," remarked Allan.

"I would agree," said Gilly, comparing the house with

the other buildings around the green. "But I quite like it being different. It stands out."

The front of the house had a minimalist design, with large windows, and walls that were perfectly rendered. Everything about it was crisp, as were the gardens. Nothing about it was conventional for a house on a traditional village green.

Eventually, the coach moved again, following the bin lorry along the country lane out of the village. After what seemed like several miles, Gilly could see the nature reserve's boundaries. The lane from the village had followed a large loop, encompassing the reserve. The coach stopped at the main road and turned right. After a few hundred yards, the reserve's entrance was in sight, but the coach stopped again at traffic lights. There were major road works before the entrance.

"I can see why the driver came through the village," said Allan. "The coach wouldn't have been able to turn left where they've dug up the road."

Allan was right, of course. In the face of a problem or a puzzle, he could always come up with a reason or a solution.

The coach drew into the large car park, with the children eager to leave and head out onto the reserve. Once the coach was empty, the teachers assembled the party near the Visitor Centre, where they were divided into groups. Some would have guides from the reserve to take them around, while the rest would be accompanied by the teachers, most of whom had visited many times before.

Gilly always enjoyed their visits to Brook Marsh. The lakes and the shallow scrapes seemed to blend into the landscape more effectively every year, and the young woodlands were developing well. The morning passed quickly, and soon it was time to eat their packed lunches.

The children were good, and took all their litter to the bins around the picnic site.

Gilly looked at her watch. She had arranged for everyone to return to the Visitor Centre at three o'clock, as the warden was going to give a talk, and then the other teachers could enjoy a drink from the café. She thought about how lucky she was to be able to come on these outings, and how things would change if and when she took over as head of a larger school, but she decided not to dwell on that today.

Early afternoon passed by far too quickly, and soon it was time to return to the Visitor Centre, and the large building dedicated to talks and lectures. The children were divided into two groups. The first group would go inside for a talk by the Warden, while the remaining group enjoyed pond dipping, and drawing pictures of things they had seen, until it was their turn for the talk.

While Gilly and Allan's group were inside with the Warden, they enjoyed cups of tea from the café. They chatted about how successful the day had been, and Allan suggested returning in the winter when the migrant birds had arrived.

It was then that Gilly's mind returned to this morning's journey, and the house on the village green. Gilly realised she could remember seeing the house before, even though she had never visited the village. Allan was talking about the bird life on the reserve when he noticed Gilly looking into space, very much removed from what he had been saying.

"Is everything OK?" he asked. "You appear to be on another planet."

It took Gilly a moment to respond, and at first what she said didn't make much sense to Allan.

"I remember the house on the green. I know who used to live there."

Gilly's words were slow. She appeared very disturbed.

"Seeing the house earlier has obviously affected you," Allan replied.

"Yes." Gilly nodded. "As a child, I wrote a story about the family who lived in that house, exactly where we stopped this morning. They had to move to a much older house, and I think something awful happened to them all." She was sounding more focused now.

"Does this have anything to do with our outing last December, in the pub? When you met the invisible man?" asked Allan.

There was a pause before Gilly replied.

"Yes, it does. The invisible man, as you call him, lived with the family in the house. He was their nephew."

"Oh, Gilly, this must be disturbing for you," said Allan.

There were two old ladies talking away on the next bench. Allan had been listening to some of their conversation and had learned they came from the village nearby. When one of them stood up and made her way to the café for another drink, Allan whispered to Gilly, "Shall I ask this lady about the house? She may be able to tell us something."

Gilly nodded.

The lady was in her seventies, smartly dressed and of slight build. Allan started chatting to her, and Gilly leaned forward to join in. He learned that they would come here once a week for a drink and a bite to eat. The lady's friend had to wait a while in the café queue, so Allan explained that they had driven through the village and noticed a very smart house on the green, giving an excellent description.

"I know the one you mean. The president of the golf club lives there," said the lady.

"Is that so?" said Allan. "I expect the house has been there a while. Has he always lived there?"

"Oh, no. The Palmers built the house. He was a builder from Bury. They took a long while. It had to be right, you know? A doctor lived there, a surgeon. They didn't mix much in the village, but they were very pleasant. Mr and Mrs Roberts."

The lady was interrupted by her friend who had returned with their drinks. When the friend had sat down, Gilly politely asked if she remembered if a family called Conway had lived there in the late sixties. The lady's whole manner changed.

"No, I can't. That's too long ago for me to remember," she said. And with that, she turned away and started talking to her friend.

Allan stood up and slowly walked away, closely followed by Gilly. When they were a distance away, Allan said, "It is strange that she could remember the builder of the house, and the Doctor for whom it was built, but not the Conways."

"When I mentioned them, she looked terrified, so whatever happened couldn't have been good," replied Gilly.

The two classes were leaving the Visitor Centre, so Gilly and Allan went to meet them. All the children had leaflets and were talking about the wildlife, and what they would be looking for while the next two classes went in to have their talk.

Everyone enjoyed coming here. The wardens were young, and engaged so well with the children. When the other classes left the talk, Gilly and Allan, along with the other teachers, assembled the children in the car park ready for the journey home. They thanked the staff for a most enjoyable day and said they would look forward to their next visit.

The coaches soon arrived and quickly filled up. Gilly wondered whether the driver would go back through the village. As the coach neared the road, she saw that the roadworks had been completed, and the driver was able to make a right turn. Perhaps this was for the best, she thought. Seeing the house this morning had disturbed her. She knew, by the ladies' reaction to her question, that this was the Conways' home, just as she had written.

Back at school, when the children had been collected, the teachers made their way to the car park, leaving only Gilly and Allan.

"Please feel free to call me if you have any more incidents, like remembering the house from your story," said Allan.

"Do you believe me, Allan?" Gilly asked. "Usually when I confide in family and friends, they try to offer me convincing explanations. But when something like this happens, I'm sure these experiences are leading me somewhere."

Allan rested his hand on her shoulder. "I believe every word. In life, so many things can't be explained, so you have to draw your own conclusions. Friends usually say what you want to hear, which isn't really much use."

"Thank you, Allan," Gilly said. "That means a lot to me."

"I must go," said Allan, looking at his watch. "Chris and I have been invited out this evening."

Gilly promised to keep Allan updated. She invited him to visit and read her story, promising to update him with the events that had happened since their evening at the pub, when she had seen Simon Newton.

Driving home, she felt reassured that Allan had been there when she had seen the house, and that he'd noticed the reaction from the lady they had spoken to. Allan believed her, and he was interested in her experiences.

Gilly had always liked Allan. Some while ago he had confided in Gilly about his partner, Chris – Chris being a man. Gilly had given him the confidence, help and support to make this known at school, and for that he would be eternally grateful.

Chapter 15

Gilly was looking forward to the half-term break. She was hoping to enjoy some days out, if the weather was fair. Perhaps she could persuade Jimmy to join her. Since taking over from his father, he seemed so keen to build the business that he had very little time for a social life. She did like Jimmy, so she decided to give him a call and invite him out. Gilly knew she would have to be firm, and insist that he took a few days off.

Gilly also planned to spend some time with her father, and enjoy the luxury of the pool and spa complex again.

The week before half term, she received a call from her mother, and all her plans changed. Her mother had made the decision to move, and asked for Gilly's help clearing out the loft. Gilly knew they would find things of sentimental value to her mother, and that she wouldn't want to ask anyone else.

It was the Tuesday morning of half-term week when Gilly arrived.

"Morning, Gilly," said her mother. "Thank you for helping me. I think we're in for a busy time!"

"This all seems very sudden, Mummy. I know you wanted to downsize eventually, but you seem to be clearing out very quickly."

"Yes, you're right, darling. I was going to do this over two or three years, but I realised that if I took that long, I may not move at all. I'd like to be ready when I find the right property to move into."

"Why don't you ask Jimmy to build a home to your specifications?" suggested Gilly. "Somewhere modern, in a good location?"

"Do you know, that is a really good idea. I could design the dimensions and the locations of the rooms to suit my needs, instead of needing disruptive alterations further down the line." Julia's response was so positive, it seemed that she couldn't wait to get going.

"Excellent, Mummy! I'll give him a call this evening and ask him to call you, and discuss your requirements."

Julia had designated the studio downstairs as the collection point for all the belongings she wanted to keep. "If I can sort personal belongings and store them in here, then I can see what furniture I would like to take with me, and the rest can be sold at Lathams." Julia's answer was definite. Her mind was made up.

"Do you have an ideal location in mind?" asked Gilly.

"Well, I would like to live on the edge of a village, perhaps with some neighbours nearby. I've loved living here, but it's off the beaten track, and too isolated. As I am getting older, I feel I need a bit of company nearby."

Julia had thought things through, and all her proposals

made sense. Gilly could see how focused her mother was, and she was pleased for her.

"Another thing, Gilly. If I had good neighbours, I could travel for weeks on end, and hopefully they would keep an eye on the place. I wouldn't have to burden you with that."

"Oh, Mummy," Gilly replied. "It's no trouble – but I can see how useful that would be."

When they had sorted through several boxes, Julia asked her daughter to stay for dinner. Gilly accepted, realising that this visit could last well into the evening. She would probably consume too much wine to be able to drive home, and end up staying over, but it was half term, so that didn't really matter.

Gilly stayed until after lunch the following day. Between them, they had managed to sort through several boxes of Julia's possessions. Julia had been definite about keeping only treasured items, so several charity shops stood to gain a number of valuable items. Gilly left feeling that her mother was absolutely right to be moving. A few more years, and the upheaval would be too much. So, while Julia's health was good, and Gilly was able to help her mother, the time was right.

Gilly arrived home ready for a rest. After sorting through the post, she made a drink and put her feet up. She knew that during the latter part of the week she would have to give some thought to the next half of term, leading up to Christmas. This was always an enjoyable time of year for the children, and several activities had already been planned. She also needed to arrange another visit to the new school site, and she decided to agree a date with Jimmy when she spoke to him about her mother's ideas for her new home.

Gilly rang Jimmy at his home later that evening and, to her surprise, he answered. He usually had to return her call, so it was nice not to have to wait to speak to him.

Jimmy was pleased to hear from her. He apologised for not being in touch for so long, as he had been so busy at work it seemed ridiculous. Jimmy listened to Gilly as she explained her mother's thoughts on moving. He said he would be more than happy to accommodate her needs, suggesting a meeting with his architect to find out how they would best be able to help.

It was then that he had an idea about the location.

"I'm actually going to view a site that might be of interest to your mother. It's a few miles away, though. Near the village of Westbrook." Jimmy seemed pleased to help.

"Is it near the nature reserve?" asked Gilly.

"No. Opposite direction, but you're in the right area," he replied.

"I'll speak to my mother and see if the area would interest her. Then perhaps we could go over and have a look."

"That sounds good. If she's interested, I'm going to visit the site in two or three weeks. I can arrange it for a weekend, and you could come with me for an initial visit. If I'm happy, we can apply for outline planning permission before involving your mother, to avoid any disappointment."

"That's an excellent idea. And we could find somewhere to have lunch out, and catch up."

Jimmy liked her idea, and said he would call to arrange a convenient date.

It was later that week when Gilly visited her father. She rang the evening before and he seemed pleased she would call in for the afternoon.

She arrived early on Friday afternoon. As before, Gilly brought her swimming costume with the intention of relaxing at the spa. As usual, after she parked and walked around the corner of the building, she found the French doors to her father's apartment unlocked, and let herself in.

"Good heavens – what a nice surprise, Gilly! Will you be staying?" her father asked.

"Yes, I hope so. It's what we arranged yesterday when I rang," said Gilly, surprised.

"Well, if you say so, my dear. However, I have no recollection of you calling."

Gilly found this strange. Her father was always so focused, and his memory was usually very sharp, but she wouldn't let this spoil the afternoon. As before, they were joined by Inge. The pool and spa complex was wonderful, and somewhere she could really unwind.

Gilly mentioned her father's loss of memory to Inge, who had noticed the same thing on several occasions.

"However," she said, "he still manages to complete a daily crossword in his newspaper."

Gilly was pleased to hear this and, although her father wasn't what Gilly considered old, she knew that age could creep up suddenly.

Her weekend was busy, preparing for the next half of term, and soon she returned to the job she enjoyed. One evening towards the end of the first week, Jimmy telephoned. He was intending to make a visit to the proposed building site in mid-November, and he asked Gilly to join him on the Sunday morning, the weekend after next. Gilly agreed, and Jimmy's offer of lunch at a nearby country pub would be too good to miss anyway. She had given the area some thought, although it was only from going to the nature reserve with school that she was familiar with that part of the county.

The village of Westbrook was pretty, and mostly unspoilt, but that house on the village green had at some time been home to the Conway family – she was sure of that. Gilly decided she would go with Jimmy, even if her mother wasn't keen on the location.

There was something there – something strange – and she felt sure that someone would know more. Perhaps this nearby pub of Jimmy's would be a good place to make some discreet enquiries. After all, people usually opened up after a few drinks.

Gilly spoke to her mother, mentioning the area of the proposed development. Julia told Gilly she would consider moving to Westbrook, and she was pleased her daughter was going with Jimmy to give her opinion.

Chapter 16

The Sunday morning came around. The weather had turned colder, with dull, drab days, and this Sunday was very foggy. It was a day made for staying at home, but it was too late to cancel now.

Jimmy picked her up in his Land Rover. Once again, he had made the effort to give it a good clean, and he, too, was looking smart in a sort of casual way. The journey seemed quick, despite the poor visibility. Jimmy was a fast driver, but even he was being careful this morning. He drove slowly through the village of Westbrook, passing the green and the house Gilly had recognised. Gilly felt her mood change, and a cold chill ran through her. She fell silent, even though Jimmy was still chatting away.

Jimmy took a left turn when leaving the village. "I think we're nearly there," he said.

"Let's hope so," Gilly replied, already regretting her decision to come along.

The lane was low, lined with tall hedges and fields at a higher level. Then came a right-hand bend with a smaller lane leading off on the left-hand side. Jimmy drove around the bend and was about to accelerate.

"You've missed the turning," Gilly said.

"Are you sure?" he replied as he slowed and stopped. "How do you know?"

Gilly remained silent, and Jimmy noticed how quiet she had become. He drove on slowly to find a gateway, and turned the car round. He headed back to the corner very slowly and stopped.

"Are you sure it's the lane we need, Gilly?"

Gilly nodded, and in a very nervous voice replied, "Definitely."

The lane was narrow. Jimmy commented that it would be difficult for delivery vehicles accessing the site. Gilly had imagined the house to be nearer the road, but the lane went on until it opened up to a large gravel drive. Before them stood Underwood House, slowly appearing out of the dense fog.

The house was exactly as Gilly had imagined when she had written her story, and this made her feel even more uneasy.

Jimmy pulled up. "What a good-sized house. Probably an old vicarage," he said.

The house looked drab, and the weather wasn't helping. Jimmy was assessing the house as a builder.

"All the climbing plants can go before they damage the render. A good paint job will add some appeal. Roughcast render looks much better coloured."

Jimmy obviously felt the house had potential, but then

he knew nothing of its history. Neither did Gilly, although she knew who had lived there, and she would like to know what had become of them.

To Gilly, the house seemed basic. A front door in the middle with windows on either side, two bedroom windows upstairs, and a chimney at each end. No quaint additions had been added over the years. No garden as such – just grass at the sides and the gravel at the front. Jimmy was leaning on the door of the Land Rover, searching in his pockets for the keys.

"Shall we go in?" he asked as he pulled out a bunch of keys.

Gilly nodded and opened her door, stepping down onto the drive. As they stood by the front door, Jimmy tried three keys before he found the right one. It was then Gilly found herself wondering whether or not to go in.

Should she, or shouldn't she?

With a start, she recognised the feeling. It was the same sensation she had experienced years ago, when she had found the doll's hand.

There could be no going back now. Perhaps the house would reveal some clues about the Conway family and Simon Newton.

She was determined to find out what had happened to them.

As they entered, they found a large hallway with stairs

on the left-hand side. Jimmy went into the room on the left, and Gilly followed.

"Have you noticed how well-kept the house is?" he asked. "No dirt or dust. It's all very clean. It's as if someone has only just moved out."

"You get that impression, but no one has lived here for many years," Gilly answered with absolute certainty.

Jimmy felt it was better not to ask too much. He had known Gilly all his life, and of late she had been behaving strangely. He knew there must be a good reason.

The two reception rooms at the front were in good order, according to Jimmy, who seemed to approve of the house. The internal décor was still in good condition, if a little dated.

As they moved through the house, Gilly felt cold. Nothing so far had given any clues about its previous occupants. There was no furniture, no old books or newspapers, and the house didn't even smell damp or musty. It all seemed very strange.

She stayed close to Jimmy as they entered the kitchen at the rear of the house. A large table stood in the centre of the room, along with six dining chairs, all bare wood. Jimmy examined each chair. Three were sturdy, but three were damaged – scratched and rickety.

Gilly felt even more uneasy. "Let's not stay too long, Jimmy." She sounded very nervous.

"We'd better look upstairs before we leave." Jimmy walked towards her and took her hand.

"This house is giving me the creeps, Jimmy. Can't you feel something is wrong?"

"It does have an atmosphere, I'll agree." He squeezed her hand tightly.

They headed slowly up the stairs, Gilly stopping on each tread.

"There's no noise. I thought all staircases creaked," said Gilly in a soft, nervous voice.

"The house has no central heating, so the wood hasn't dried and shrunk," replied Jimmy, calmly.

When they reached the landing, Gilly tightened her grip on Jimmy's hand. They moved slowly to the bedroom at the front, on the left-hand side of the house. Jimmy opened the door.

Even before Gilly had seen inside the room, in a low voice she said, "This was Simon's room."

"I see," replied Jimmy.

He could tell something was wrong. This wasn't the bold, confident girl he had known all his life. Once again there was no furniture, no curiosities or carpets – just wooden floorboards.

"I like the colour, Gilly." Jimmy pointed out the sage green colour of the walls, now somewhat faded.

"He had good taste," was Gilly's only reply.

Jimmy examined the window, and then they moved across the landing to the room on the right of the house. They entered. Jimmy let go of Gilly's hand and knelt down by the fireplace to look up into the chimney. Gilly knew that this had been Mark and Daphne's room. The patterned floral wallpaper was faded, and there were no clues here. No furniture, no paintings on the walls.

"Someone looks after this place. There are no cobwebs," said Jimmy, standing up. "But I think you're right, Gilly. No one has lived here for years."

"Something happened in this house. No one will live here. It's obvious."

Her voice was still faint, and she had returned to Jimmy's side. If she was right, it would be a pointless purchase. However, Jimmy was more interested in the land that went with the house.

Back on the landing, Jimmy headed towards the room to the rear. He flung open a door.

"A good-sized bathroom," he remarked. Gilly peered inside. From where she stood, everything was spotless. "People could move in straight away," said Jimmy.

"So, why haven't they?" Gilly asked. "Something is very wrong here, Jimmy. Please don't buy the house, or the land."

He could tell she was disturbed, and nodded to show his concern. It was then that Gilly froze. She stood still, by the bathroom door, and Jimmy realised they would soon have to leave.

"I'd like to view the last room, Gilly, and then I promise we can go."

He took Gilly's hand and they slowly walked towards the bedroom on the right. Gilly could feel her hands shaking as Jimmy opened the door.

This was Emma's room. She just knew horrific things had happened in here, but instead of staying on the landing, she followed Jimmy in. She could feel a horrible atmosphere. She wanted to run away, and leave the house at once.

The room was icy cold, but she felt there might be clues here to what had happened. She held onto Jimmy, who had fallen silent.

"You must feel something here, Jimmy," she said in a low, nervous voice.

Jimmy nodded and squeezed her hand.

"Let's go," he replied.

The pair had hardly stepped through the door, and to Jimmy's surprise, Gilly led him into the middle of the room. This room was like all the others, but the floorboards in the centre had depressions in them. Several, as if they had been hit with a hammer.

Gilly was shaking. "Get me away from here now, Jimmy."

Her voice was terrified and she was pulling on his arm as they hastily left the room. She ran across the landing and down the stairs, leaving him to close the door. Jimmy followed, and made his way to the front of the house. He could see that Gilly was already sitting in his Land Rover – he had forgotten to lock the car, as usual.

The weather hadn't improved. If anything, the fog seemed even more dense as Jimmy drove away down the lane.

"I imagine the land adjoining the house is over there," said Jimmy, as he looked to his right.

Gilly made no comment. All she wanted was to get away as soon as possible.

He turned right onto the road leaving Underwood House. Gilly decided she would never return, and she hoped Jimmy would not pursue the purchase. They seemed to drive for miles along country lanes. Gilly wished they were heading for home, but she knew Jimmy was intent on finding the country pub that had been recommended.

Chapter 17

E ventually the Kenston village sign appeared.

"I think we've come the long way round," said Jimmy. "I'm sure we're only about six miles away from the house."

Gilly remained silent. From what she could see, the village appeared to be very pretty, with old cottages and well-kept gardens. Jimmy slowed down when he spotted the sign for the Fox Inn. He turned into the car park at the side, only to find all the spaces were taken.

"That's a good sign," he commented. "It must be worth a visit!"

Gilly rather hoped there would be no room, and that they would have to go home. Jimmy reversed back and parked directly in front of the inn. It was a picturesque building, with pink rendered walls, climbing plants, and in the centre a wooden porch to the door, all under an ageing thatched roof.

Gilly didn't feel like sitting with people. She certainly wouldn't be good company, but Jimmy seemed determined to have his lunch. As he opened the door, they could see that all of the tables were full, and it was a real squeeze to get to the bar. Jimmy, being well-built, pushed through the drinkers as though he was in a rugby scrum. He ordered two drinks from the lady who was serving, and asked her if there was any chance of them having lunch.

She grinned. "If you can find a table."

Jimmy looked around and noticed a small table in the corner by the front window. There was an old man sitting on a chair reading a newspaper. He wore a tatty jacket and an old cap pulled well down on his forehead.

"How about over there?" said Jimmy pointing in his direction.

The lady shrugged. "Sit with Old Ray if you dare," she said.

Jimmy shrugged his shoulders and ordered two roast lunches, paid, and took Gilly's hand, making for the table. Gilly had made up her mind that this was a bad idea. When they reached the corner, Jimmy asked the old man whether he would mind if they joined him.

There was a loud, disapproving grunt, so obviously he did. Jimmy pulled the chair away from the table ready for Gilly to sit down. As she sat, she drew the chair further away to distance herself from Old Ray. Jimmy sat down.

"I wish we could just go home, Jimmy. That house has made me feel sick. If you only knew the feelings I was having there, you might understand."

By now Jimmy had finished his first pint, while Gilly had only started her gin. Jimmy noticed that the old man's glass was empty, and as he went to get up asked, "Would you like another, sir?"

With that, the old man shoved the glass in Jimmy's direction without even looking up from his paper, and said in a loud, gruff voice, "Bitter."

Jimmy took both glasses and headed for the bar. This infuriated Gilly. This Old Ray character hadn't even made eye contact, only grunted, and now when her friend was good enough to offer him a drink, he couldn't even say 'yes, please'. No doubt there would be no 'thank you' either.

He needed to be told his behaviour was not acceptable. He needed to be taught some manners. Oh, yes, she was going to give him a good verbal dressing-down. He would feel like a schoolboy when she was done. Gilly was about to open her mouth when the old man spoke.

"Must have been to Underwood House," he said, in a deep voice.

Gilly was taken back. He had obviously been listening to their conversation, and knew her feelings.

"Yes, you're right."

Gilly was about to carry on when Jimmy returned with the drinks, and she was surprised when Old Ray did thank him.

When Jimmy was seated, Gilly said, "This gentleman knows the house we've seen."

Jimmy looked in Ray's direction. "What can you tell

us about Underwood House then, sir?"

Old Ray started his drink before he replied.

"People have died there. Died in a most horrific way." He paused. "I'd say within the last twenty to thirty years or so."

"I think you're right, and I'm guessing this has happened in the large bedroom at the back," Gilly said, quietly.

Ray nodded. "I carried out repairs to the sash windows. Couldn't even stay in the room. I worked from the outside."

With that, a waitress arrived with their lunches. Jimmy was delighted and started to tuck in. Gilly was slow to start, and was more interested in getting as much information from Ray as she could.

"Do you know who last lived there?" Gilly asked.

"I don't," he replied. "I've only lived here for five years, and anyone I've asked seems too nervous to say anything." Ray had finished his drink and placed his newspaper in his jacket pocket. He was clearly looking to leave, but Gilly was keen to find out all she could before he left.

"One last thing, Ray," she said. "Who looks after the house? Only we've noticed how clean and well-kept it is for an empty property."

"The vicar, Reverend Jacobs. He keeps things in order," was Ray's reply.

"That seems a strange thing for a priest to do, surely." Gilly looked puzzled.

"He's no ordinary vicar. He's something else. Ask any-one." With that, and without even saying goodbye, Old Ray made his way to the door and left.

Gilly felt better. She continued with her lunch – roast pork, which was superb. She no longer felt that the strange events she had experienced were coincidental. She was sure that they were all linked. It was if they were clues in a puzzle – a puzzle waiting for her to sort out. By now, Jimmy had finished his lunch and drink, and was at the bar ordering a dessert. Gilly declined, as she was still enjoying her rather large first course.

Reverend Jacobs. He would know all about Underwood House and its secrets. She knew her mother would be able to ask him, as she had known him for many years, supplying flowers for weddings and funerals at his church.

Jimmy returned, and was soon presented with a large chocolate fudge cake.

"We should come here again," he said with a smile. "The food is excellent."

It was as if he had completely forgotten about Gilly's reaction to the house.

The pair left soon afterwards. Gilly thanked him for the tasty lunch, but she was keen to return home.

"I will find out what happened in that house, Jimmy. I really hope you aren't planning to buy it, or the land that comes with it." Gilly spoke very firmly.

"It has lost its appeal, now we know it has such an unpleasant history," he replied.

Jimmy parked beside Gilly's car. The bleak afternoon was becoming dark.

"Would you care for a coffee then, Jimmy?"

He accepted. As they sat at the kitchen table, he did seem concerned as to how she was feeling.

"I think it was meant to be that we had lunch in The Fox," Gilly said. "I didn't want to, after our visit to the house. I wanted you to bring me home, but I knew you would want your lunch. Meeting Old Ray was the tonic I needed. I didn't like him and was about to really tell him off. But when he told us how he had been affected by the house, I realised we had a great deal in common."

Jimmy finished his coffee. He asked if Gilly was feeling well enough for him to leave.

"You go, Jimmy," she replied. "I need to prepare for tomorrow and I'll need to give my mother a call. So, thank you – I'll be fine."

Chapter 18

After he had left, she sat for a while, thinking of everything that had happened since meeting Simon nearly a year ago. Today she had visited his home. Was this where he had lost his life? Of that she wasn't sure. However, she was certain that the Conways had died there. How and why? That would be for her to find out.

But what if it was dangerous to do so? After all, Old Ray did mention that people were reluctant to speak about the residents, as were the ladies when she spoken to them at the nature reserve.

Later that afternoon she called her mother and mentioned her visit to Underwood House. She didn't say how it had affected her, or what Old Ray had said, only that someone at the pub had told them the house had a very dark secret. She explained that Reverend Jacobs looked after the place.

Julia agreed to speak to the Reverend, as she knew him well, but told her daughter not to raise her hopes too much. She had known Linden Jacobs for many years, and she knew he would only tell her as much as he wanted her to know.

Julia kept her word, and later the following week

she called Linden Jacobs. At the weekend, she rang her daughter and let her know what she had found out – or rather what she hadn't.

"I told him that you and Jimmy had visited Underwood House, then had lunch at the local pub, and that someone there had mentioned the house's history," Julia explained. "Linden assured me that during his time in the area nothing terrible had happened there. However, he pointed out that all old houses have their secrets, and he expects that people will have died there over the years. As for the house being empty for so long, he explained that it had been used for storage. He's only recently had it cleared it out, which it why it appeared so well-kept."

Julia paused, and Gilly waited for her mother to continue.

"I can't shake the feeling that he did know more," she admitted. "But he wasn't prepared to reveal too much information. Whether I can try again at a later date … we shall see."

Gilly thanked her mother for trying and said she would see her soon. As she put the phone down, there was a knock at the door.

"Hello, Jimmy," she said with a smile as she opened the door. "Good to see you."

"I wanted to find out how you are, first of all." He seemed genuinely concerned.

"I'm still very troubled – but I am determined to find out what went on at Underwood House."

"Well, I wanted to let you know that I have no intention of purchasing the house, or the adjoining land," Jimmy explained. "Firstly, because of your reaction, and also a couple of the guys who work for me know the old boy we saw in the pub. His name is Ray Barker, and in the past he has been spot-on with his suspicions about properties that have been hard to sell."

"I'm really relieved to hear that. Thank you, Jimmy. All I have to do now is find out exactly what happened there, and why."

"Please be careful, Gilly. There must be a reason people won't talk about what happened."

"I'll be discreet, and I am patient – but I promise you, Jimmy, I will find out who is responsible for whatever happened at Underwood House."

Gilly knew she needed to find someone who had known the Conway family at the time they lived there. That would be her next move.

Gilly decided to tell Allan about her experience at Underwood House, and about having her feelings confirmed by Ray Barker over lunch at the pub. When she saw him in the staff room, she asked if he could spare some time for her later on. Allan was pleased to oblige, and suggested meeting up after school later that day. They met in her classroom when all the children had gone home.

Gilly gave Allan a very detailed account of how the day had unfolded. She explained the feelings she'd had in the house, and how these were the same as Ray Barker's, even though they had only just met.

Allan listened in silence until Gilly had finished.

"Well, it certainly seems that you're onto something. I have no doubt that you sensed something in the house, and then to hear that someone else had a similar experience? Yes, you're right to try and find out more." He paused for a short while before revealing that he, too, had some news.

"Chris's parents joined us for lunch recently. They live near Westbrook. I mentioned the house on the green to see if they might know who lived there. First of all, his mother said she had no idea about its residents, but then his father mentioned there had been a family who lived there who had to move on. Chris's mother wasn't pleased when he spoke, telling her husband it was a long while ago and it should be left alone. However, he was determined to tell me what he knew. He then went on to say they had moved to a large, remote house a mile or two from the village."

"This is all very positive, Allan! Thank you. Do you think I could meet them?"

"I don't think so," Allan replied. "He was in enough trouble by the time they left. Chris was really annoyed with me for bringing it up. I think he's probably told me everything he knows. However, he did remember the daughter being a very pretty girl, who attracted a lot of interest among the young men."

"Did he tell you her name?" asked Gilly.

"No names were mentioned, and the local lads were all disappointed, as she was only interested in older men. Older men with money who would spoil her – which according to Chris's father, they certainly did."

Gilly thanked Allan very much for finding out what he had. She would find out the truth, however long it took. After all, the clues had been waiting since she'd written her story.

During the evening, Gilly received a call from her mother, asking whether she had made any plans for Christmas. Gilly questioned her mother's reason for asking, as they both usually went out to a lovely country hotel with several of their friends.

"Well, darling, I thought this year we could change our plans. You see, your father doesn't seem very well at the moment. It's his memory. I saw him at the weekend, and we both feel that Christmas together seems a good idea while he still knows who we are. I'm not saying things are that serious yet, but it seems like the right thing to do."

Julia's suggestion had come out of the blue. Gilly wouldn't have thought her mother still cared about him, so she was pleasantly surprised at the idea of being with both her parents at Christmas. She was also very concerned that his memory was deteriorating, and she understood the doctors were still looking for reasons for his condition. Gilly agreed to change the plans for Christmas, and in the meantime she decided to visit her father more often.

Chapter 19

The year had passed very quickly. Her plan to visit the new school building with the children for a second time had not come about, so she decided to talk to Jimmy about a visit early in the new year. That would give them all something to look forward to after the excitement of Christmas. She also hoped to spend some time over the holidays with Jimmy, so she could make the arrangements then.

Gilly was pleased to break up for Christmas. The previous few weeks had been extremely busy, and she was feeling drained. She had visited her father when she could, but it was usually after lunchtime, and she always found him sleeping or very drowsy. As yet the doctors hadn't confirmed his condition, and he was due to see a specialist at the local hospital just before Christmas.

With everything that was going on, she still thought about her visit to Underwood House, and she asked Jimmy if anyone had made an offer for the house and land. Jimmy told her that no one seemed interested, which he thought was strange. Gilly, however, could fully understand.

On Christmas morning, Gilly collected her mother. The day was cold and bright. For several years, they had stopped buying presents for each other, and instead gave generous donations to a local charity. As they drove along, Julia said she had spoken to her husband on Christmas Eve. He had received a diagnosis for his condition, and he would tell them about it today.

Gilly parked as usual outside her father's window. Today, they entered through the main front doors. The entrance hall looked magnificent, with a huge tree, very tastefully lit and decorated. The staff were, as always, delightful, and wished the pair a happy Christmas. On reaching Charles's apartment door, Julia gave two knocks. After a moment, the nurse opened the door and let them in.

Rachel, his nurse, and had been with him since the home had opened. She was a slight lady with dark hair and very good looks.

"I'll leave you alone for a while," she said, after the usual Christmas greetings.

Charles was sitting in his chair. He had a big smile on his face and welcomed them both.

"Would you care for a drink?" he asked.

"Just a small one before lunch, then. How about you, darling?" Julia's glanced towards her daughter.

"I'm fine, thank you, Mummy. No drink for me today. I'm driving."

Julia mixed herself a large gin and tonic.

"We'll have some coffee then, Gilly." said Charles. "Perhaps you could be kind and make some." Gilly noticed on her way to the kitchen that the dining room table was laid for lunch, which seemed unusual. Normally on such occasions they would eat in the large dining room, with the home's many other residents. After all, everyone who lived there needed Charles's approval before they were allowed to move in, and there was a very friendly atmosphere. Gilly returned with two coffees and sat down with her parents.

"Are we having lunch here today, Daddy?" she asked, as she passed her father his coffee.

"Yes. I felt we needed some time to ourselves. I do have some news on my condition, but let's enjoy our lunch first."

Charles was very definite about what he wanted. They sat and talked until the staff came in and served lunch – a good, traditional turkey and all of the trimmings, followed by Christmas pudding. The meal was superb – even better than the country house restaurant where they usually dined on Christmas day.

They retired to Charles's lounge to enjoy more coffee.

"You must have a drink, Gilly. A liqueur, perhaps," insisted Charles.

"No, thank you, Daddy. As I explained before, I need to drive home, so I shall decline."

Charles looked puzzled and gave a grunt.

"Well, Charles, you have some news for us about your condition?" Julia was keen to know about her husband's health.

Charles leaned back in his chair.

"I'm finding I have difficulty with remembering, concentrating. I can no longer carry out even the small amount of work that I'm used to doing. My doctors have diagnosed a mild cognitive impairment. I find this most frustrating, but there is no cure, and at present I can only accept the way I am. What I fear most is if I go on to develop dementia with a complete loss of memory."

Charles was very calm and showed no emotion about what he had revealed.

"Aren't you worried, Daddy? You don't seem to be upset at all," asked Gilly.

"I can't do anything about it, so I shall try and live my life the best as I can. You know that life is good here. I will be well looked after. My affairs are all in order, but I do have one request." Charles looked at his wife and then his daughter.

"I know you want to see us more often."

Charles nodded to Julia's reply.

"I'll visit every week, Daddy. Not just drop in. Maybe even more often."

Charles smiled at his daughter's suggestion. Julia made no such commitment, only saying how sorry she was to hear about his condition.

The afternoon passed quickly. They talked a lot about the past, and Charles really did seem to be in very good spirits. Gilly popped out about at around three o'clock to have a stroll in the gardens. She felt sad that her father may end up not being able to recognise her, but it hadn't come to that yet, and she would keep a close eye on him.

The afternoon was clear and bright. The temperature had dropped, and Gilly was pleased to return to the warmth of her father's apartment. They stayed until late afternoon, and only left when Charles needed to have his rest.

Gilly had to remove a thin coat of frost from her windscreen, and wait until the glass inside had demisted. It was a quiet journey back to her mother's house, with both of them deep in thought about the news they had received. Driving along the country lanes seemed very eerie. Not seeing any other cars was strange, and the branches of the trees which overhung the road were beginning to look white with frost. As they turned into the long drive to Julia's old farmhouse, it felt even more remote than usual.

"Mummy, I am concerned about you living out here in the sticks. You hear of terrible things happening. Now I wish you would hurry up and move."

"I wouldn't be too concerned, darling. I have always been able to look after myself," Julia answered her daughter firmly.

Gilly parked and they were both pleased to go inside. The house was warm, and Julia had left all the lights on. Once they had settled down for the evening, Gilly was at last able to enjoy a festive drink. She was planning to stay overnight, or possibly longer, if she could. They spoke about Charles, and how well he had taken the news of his diagnosis.

Boxing Day was cold and frosty, and the skies were clear with brilliant sunshine. After breakfast, Gilly decided to go for a walk. There were endless footpaths through the surrounding fields, which she could follow for miles if she wished. Julia declined the offer to join her, saying she would make a nice lunch ready for her return.

As Gilly left, she walked past the barn, which had been converted for her mother's floristry.

That's where I found the doll's hand, in a small chest.

The memory was as clear as if it had been yesterday.

As she walked through the woods, she thought about her father, and how his life would change. She also thought about all the things that had happened in the last year that couldn't be explained. How her childhood story became true, and how these events had affected her. And now, to find out that her father would lose his mind? It was yet another knock for her. Somehow, he was connected to all of this. She felt sure of that.

As she walked around the edges of the fields she began to understand why her mother hadn't moved. The countryside was beautiful – unspoilt and peaceful. Gilly knew that the next year would be challenging, with her new position as head of the school. The building was well ahead of schedule. If her mother found a smaller home, she would help as much as she could with the move. And now she realised, with making the most of the time with her father, there wouldn't be much time left for herself.

As she took a track that would lead back to the farmhouse, she realised that this was what she enjoyed. Fresh air, open space, and walking. She must do it more often. Perhaps she could persuade Jimmy to join her. He was good company, and had recently acquired a labrador, so walking would be essential for him.

As the house came into view, she noticed smoke rising straight up into the air from the chimney. Her mother had lit the huge stove in the lounge, as she usually did. Gilly opened the gate from the field into the garden and strolled around the borders. It had been a long time since she had had a good walk around, so now seemed a good time to see what her mother had been up to. As she strolled along, she came to a shady corner. Her mother had been cutting back the shade-loving plants, and had stopped before a piece of stone set into the ground.

Gilly crouched down and reached out to touch the stone, remembering its significance. This was where her beloved dog was buried. She pulled away ivy, which was partly covering the stone, to reveal the name, 'Lola.' What a dear and loving friend she had been when Gilly was growing up, and how she wished there was a dog in her life now. If only she were not so busy.

As Gilly was about to stand, she gave the stone a gentle stroke. As she did, she felt a soft, moist feeling on the back of her neck that made her jump. She looked around, but there was no one there. The feeling was exactly like being licked by Lola, all those years ago. She stood up and checked the garden, but found that she was alone. It was just another strange experience that couldn't be explained.

Gilly made her way back to the house to find her mother busy in the kitchen. Julia was nearly ready to serve another excellent roast lunch, so her timing was perfect. Julia noticed that her daughter had been quiet since returning from her walk. As they sat down to eat, she asked why, and Gilly replied that while walking she had been thinking deeply about her father, and how the future would be difficult for all of them.

After lunch and clearing up, they sat in the lounge, relaxing by the stove. This was real comfort, Gilly thought. Much better than her apartment's central heating, although realistically she knew she didn't have time to tend to a real fire. During the evening, Gilly was much more talkative, and they stayed up late watching television and enjoying gin and tonics. The following morning, Gilly left soon after breakfast.

She spent the rest of the festive season on her school work, getting ready for the new term. Her plans to go on long country walks with Jimmy and his dog didn't happen. When she had called to arrange something, he hadn't sounded at all well. He'd said it felt like flu, and he had forbidden any visitors. However, he promised to call and collect her when he was better.

He also told her what an excellent companion his dog had become, and how caring for her had changed his life. This reminded Gilly of Lola, and the strange experience she'd had in her mother's garden.

Whatever happened there? she wondered.

New Year's Eve was a low-key event. Usually, her colleagues from school met up at a local pub, but this year several had caught the flu. Instead, she stayed at home and celebrated with a few of her neighbours.

Gilly usually visited her father twice a week. He remained in good spirits, although he did become frustrated when he could no longer complete the crossword in the daily newspaper.

Back at school in the new year she had to cover for several teachers who were still recovering from their illness. With the extra teaching, and visits to her father, she found, as expected, that there wasn't much spare time for herself. Her mother was still keen to move, but this wouldn't happen until the summer, or so Julia hoped.

Chapter 20

Towards the end of January, Julia returned home one afternoon to a message on her answerphone. When she listened, it was hard to believe whose voice it was. Reverend Jacobs was asking her to call him, but it sounded nothing like his usual voice. He did mention he had been unwell, so that might explain the difference. He asked her to call either late morning or very early afternoon, as he had to rest, and mustn't be disturbed.

The next day around mid-morning Julia called the Reverend. As in his message, he sounded slow and older. He asked if she would be good enough to visit him very soon. Julia agreed, and arranged to see him the next day, then she asked about his health. He revealed that he had recently suffered a massive heart attack, and wasn't expected to live much longer. He told her he should have remained in hospital, but he had insisted on spending what time he had left at home. Under the care of a good nurse, this was arranged.

The following morning Julia arrived at Westbrook Rectory around eleven o'clock. Reverend Jacobs hadn't mentioned his reasons for asking to see Julia, but she assumed he had some information to pass on. Julia was greeted at the door by his nurse, a very pleasant young lady with a pretty face and blonde hair. She introduced herself as Marie and explained that Reverend Jacobs needed as much rest as possible.

"He can talk for a while, then usually he falls asleep. Please allow him to sleep, but feel free to stay until he wakes again. He does have important information for you. I'll knock before I enter the lounge so as not to disturb you, but you can call me at any time. I know his time is short."

Marie was definite and to the point as she showed Julia to the lounge.

Julia walked towards Linden and touched his hand.

"My dear friend," she said, gently. "How it saddens me to see you this way."

She had known him ever since her floristry shop opened. He had always recommended her when flower arrangements were needed for the church, although she didn't know him well personally. He asked her to sit down and requested coffee from Marie. Julia moved a chair so she was sitting just in front of him.

"I shan't live for long," he said. "The last time we spoke you were asking about Underwood House, and your daughter's reaction during her visit."

Julia nodded. She knew he had known more than he had shared.

"Yes," she replied. "She has been troubled for some while, and the visit to Underwood House affected her deeply."

"I shall tell you everything I know, on the understanding that you will not mention anything to your daughter until I have passed away."

Linden closed his eyes for a few minutes, only to be disturbed by Marie bringing the coffee. Julia sat patiently as Linden took a sip from his cup.

"I will say nothing until after your funeral. I promise you that," said Julia.

Linden gave her a brief smile before continuing.

"Now, a family by the name of Conway were the last residents of Underwood House. Mike and Daphne, who had a daughter, Emma, and also took care of an orphaned nephew, Simon Newton." He paused for a sip of coffee. Their names were familiar, Julia realised – exactly the ones Gilly had mentioned. "They came to live there after losing their house – a rather large, smart property on the green at Westbrook." He paused again.

"You say they lost their house. How did that happen?" asked Julia.

"Well, Mike Conway had a gambling addiction, and a very serious one. He was in debt to a ruthless gang of men who took his house to clear the debt."

"Surely people can't do that, Linden," Julia protested.

"Oh, those people can," said Linden, nodding.

He rested for a while, falling asleep for around twenty minutes. When he stirred, Julia asked if he felt well enough to continue, and he nodded.

"I will go on. Daphne Conway was secretary to Bishop Donald, my boss. She was very distraught at work. When the bishop learned of the situation, he offered her Underwood House. After all, it was only used for shooting parties in winter. The only rent he asked was for her to work a few more hours every week.

"The Conways moved in, and made the place their own. Initially they disliked living in such a remote location, but they grew to enjoy the peace and quiet it offered. Gradually, with Daphne in charge of the finances, they were once again able to enjoy a good lifestyle. Emma left school and took a job in the nearby town. As for Simon, he was very clever, and a very talented artist.

"They very much kept themselves to themselves. It was Simon who was different. Both Helen, my wife, and I liked him very much, and he became a good friend."

Julia could tell he was tiring and suggested they take a break. Linden nodded before drifting off once more. Julia collected the coffee mugs and took them through to the kitchen, where she found Marie.

"I've left him resting. Perhaps I should go and return another time," suggested Julia.

"Let him rest. I'll make him some lunch. You're welcome to stay as well – I know he wanted to pass this information on, and I'm afraid he could pass away at any time."

Julia could see that Marie was right. She would stay all afternoon if necessary. After lunch, Linden seemed much brighter and stronger.

"Now, where was I?" he said, in a deep voice.

"You were telling me about Simon, and how much you liked him," Julia reminded Linden.

"Ah, yes. Daphne was the bishop's secretary, very efficient and hardworking. He relied on her very much and trusted her totally. One day, the bishop had to leave the office in a hurry, leaving books and papers on his desk, which was unheard of. He also left the safe open, which even Daphne wasn't allowed to access. Before he left, he asked Daphne to tidy things for him. She obliged, and was ready to close the safe, but she found it irresistible to take a look through some of the papers and documents inside.

"Mostly, the contents were as she expected, but one large, thick envelope seemed out of place. Checking inside, she found documents regarding their former house, which had been taken to pay off her husband's gambling debt, along with the names of the men who Mike owed so much money to. She found other business interests they were involved with as well – all very suspicious and secretive.

"Knowing that the bishop might be involved enraged Daphne. With evidence in her hands showing who else was involved, she made copies of the contents of the envelope. She intended to blackmail them all while threatening them with exposure."

Linden paused and took a sip of water, while Julia asked if there was anything he wanted. He shook his head. "Only to rest for a few moments," was his reply.

Julia sat back in her chair while Linden once more fell asleep. She wondered what she was about to hear next.

"This will be difficult for you, Julia." Linden opened his eyes and reached for his glass, taking several large sips.

"Will it? I wonder why?" she responded.

After a long pause Linden continued.

"The men who Mike Conway owed money to were known as the Formidable Four." Linden paused once more.

"Oh, my God. My husband's involved in this," breathed Julia, as she remembered her husband and his colleagues. She knew they were ruthless, greedy men who would stop at nothing to get their way.

"You're right, Julia. Charles was involved, as was Marcus Kennedy, the Chief Constable of the police force. So you see, they really could get away with anything. The bishop was involved. He was well connected, and a lifelong friend of the others. In his defence, he used his financial gains to help others, and to contribute to the maintenance of the church buildings."

Julia was shaken to hear of her husband's activities, although not entirely surprised.

"How about the fourth member, Geoffrey Payne?" she

asked.

"He was bad. Sadistic. Not someone to get involved with. He was a great womaniser and he could be charming. He was the owner of the casino where Mike Conway used to gamble. As you know, he was also a car dealer. On the surface, they all appeared to be professional, decent men. However, when they were together, they were lethal."

Julia could see Linden was tiring.

"Please have a rest," she said. "I have a lot to take in."

Linden nodded before drifting off, leaving Julia to wonder exactly what these men were capable of.

Marie popped into the lounge to see how her patient was.

"Maybe I should leave and come back tomorrow, if that's convenient," Julia said in a soft voice.

Marie shook her head. "Providing he rests often, you should stay. I know he'll be happier once you've heard what he has to say."

A short while later, Linden woke.

"I'm pleased that you're still here," he said, softly. "I'll continue."

"If you're sure, Linden. In your own time," Julia replied.

"Returning to the Conways. Both Daphne and Mike were serious about making financial demands, and blackmailing the Formidable Four. It was Emma who was cautious regarding their approach. You see, Emma worked in your husband's office, so she knew who they were dealing with. Daphne and Mike managed to convince her, showing her the information they had.

"They compiled letters with their demands. They stated that any revenue made from the men's activities should be split five ways instead of four. They also demanded ownership of Underwood House and the land adjoining it. The letters were sent, and they heard nothing.

"However, the four men met. They were enraged, and had no intention of meeting the demands. A few weeks passed, and the Conways heard nothing. I know the bishop carried on as normal, and made no mention of receiving their letter. I believe Daphne felt very uneasy working for him during this time.

"The four knew exactly what would happen – and this, I'm afraid, isn't very pleasant. They knew the Conways kept themselves to themselves, didn't mix much, and, to their knowledge, had no immediate relatives. They did their research. No one would miss the Conways – they were sure of that. Simon was spending much more time with Helen and myself, even staying with us several nights each week. He was studying for his A levels, and found he could concentrate better with us than he could at home. The bishop was aware of this arrangement, and when he asked whether it could be made permanent, I knew something was about to happen. Shortly after this conversation I received an order – something I bitterly disagreed with."

There was a short pause before he continued.

"I was given a date in November. In the evening, I was to go to Underwood House. I would find a Land Rover on the drive. The house would be left open. On no account was Simon to go home around this time. In the large bedroom to the rear of the house on the right-hand side, I would find three bodies. I was to load them into the Land Rover and dispose of them so they were never traced."

Julia felt sick. Very sick. She knew her husband was ruthless and greedy, as were his friends, but to have a family murdered was unthinkable.

"You went along with this, Linden?" Julia's tone was harsh.

Linden nodded. "I did. At first I refused. I had no wish to be involved. However, the bishop was very keen to remind me how Helen had been looked after when she became ill. As you may remember, she needed surgery, and treatment afterward, and then we enjoyed several more years together. This was private care she received. The very best, and it happened immediately after her diagnosis, all funded by the bishop.

"So you see, I couldn't decline his request, as much as I wanted to. As and when Helen might need further care, I needed to know it would be available. I agreed, on the understanding that Simon could attend university and train to be an architect, as he wanted."

Linden rested his head on the back of the chair as if he were about to sleep again.

"Who carried out the murders?" asked Julia, moving closer to Linden.

For a moment he had closed his eyes, but hearing Julia's voice he replied.

"No one is really sure. All I do know was that the bodies were in an awful state. The Conways suffered considerably before they died."

Julia was not convinced he couldn't reveal who the killers were, but she knew he was tiring.

"One last thing, Linden," she said. "How were the disappearances explained locally, and what became of Simon?"

"Firstly, a story was created that the Conways had family in Canada. Locals were led to believe it had always been their intention to go out and join them. However, following a bereavement, this happened sooner than expected. As they kept themselves to themselves, no one disbelieved the story.

"Simon was different. I couldn't lie to him. He was far too clever. After I had cleared up at Underwood House, we went to collect his things. As we entered the house, he looked at me and said, 'I know they're dead, Linden. I know they knew too much'. That was all he said.

"However, it was a long while before he returned to his usual self. He found he could enjoy life with us both. We never mentioned the Conways, and neither did he. He received excellent grades and then trained to be an architect, working with a local practice."

Julia knew she would have to leave soon, and let Linden rest, but she was keen to know more about Simon.

"So what became of Simon?" she asked, softly.

"Simon loved being outdoors. At university he made friends with some lads who enjoyed climbing.

Mountaineering, I suppose. They asked if he would like to join them. He agreed, but only after seeking our approval. Neither of us was keen on the idea, but who were we to stand in his way? We asked to meet his friends and see where they would be climbing, and also who would be training Simon. After meeting his friends and knowing they were all receiving professional training, I rang their instructor and spoke at length about the climbs they would be making and the locations they would be going to. We were as confident as we could be.

"Simon loved climbing. He appeared to be a natural. He would be collected by one of his friends every three to four weeks. He really enjoyed life.

"Then after about eighteen months, while climbing in Derbyshire, he fell to his death. This was devastating for both of us – Helen especially, and something she never got over. She was never the same."

Linden closed his eyes once more.

Julia knew it was time to leave. It wouldn't be fair to ask any more questions, much as she would like to. There was a knock on the door, and Marie entered the room.

"I'll leave now. He seems very tired," said Julia.

"Please let him sleep. I'll say goodbye for you. He will understand, I can assure you."

"Thank you, Marie. I'd like to call in again, if possible."

"Now that he's spoken to you, I think he'll pass away peacefully. In my experience, it will happen very soon," replied Marie.

Julia nodded, asking Marie to call her when he passed away.

"I shall," the nurse replied.

Julia found she had plenty to think about during her drive home. She thought of her husband, his colleagues, and their greed, and how no one could interfere in their plans – and what would happen if they did. Were the Conways the only ones to disappear? How would she ever find out? She had so many questions, but the only person to ask would be her husband. She doubted he would reveal anything, especially now he could blame his condition for any lack of memory.

Then she thought of her daughter. How could she tell

her? It couldn't be until after Linden's funeral, but exactly how much she would reveal she wasn't sure. Gilly thought a great deal of her father, but this would change if she knew everything he had done. Still, she had a few weeks to consider how, and how much, to tell.

After arriving home, Julia felt drained. She made herself a cup of tea before running a hot bath, followed by an early night. As she came down the stairs after a lie-in the next morning, her phone started to ring. It was Marie, letting her know that Linden had passed away peacefully in the early hours of the morning. It wasn't a surprise. Julia thanked Marie for all the care she had given him, and for looking after her yesterday. Marie said she would be attending his funeral and hoped to see Julia there. It was a sad loss for anyone who had known him. He was well-liked and respected in the area, and Julia would certainly miss him.

Chapter 21

Gilly was pleased when half term arrived – not because she had made any plans, but because it had been a hectic time at school. So many teachers had been away with illness, and it had been a miracle that Gilly had remained healthy. The weather for the half-term break was exceptional – brilliant sunshine, and exceptionally mild. She knew it wouldn't last, so it would be a good time to get out and about.

On the Tuesday, Gilly was invited to have lunch with Allan and his partner, Chris. She was looking forward to this very much. Chris was a chef, and his food was exceptional.

They lived near the village of Westbrook, in the area near the nature reserve, not far from the infamous Underwood House. Gilly had chosen her route carefully so as not to pass the corner where the track led to the house. The unpleasant experience was still in her mind, and she suspected it would remain there forever.

Allan and Chris were excellent hosts, and the food was as exceptional as the company. Gilly left the pair at around three o'clock and retraced her route home. As she drove along, she passed the parish church – only now the lane was lined with cars parked all along the verge. She had to drive carefully to avoid them, and it was then she noticed her mother's car. Julia had not mentioned anything about visiting Westbrook, which was unusual. As she made her way past the church she noticed a hearse by the gateway. Of course, she realised. People had gathered for a funeral – but whose?

She noticed everyone standing around in the church-yard, so she assumed this must be a burial. She drove slowly on, and then felt a need to return when everyone had left.

Why? She didn't know.

After the junction, Gilly pulled into the wide gateway of a field to wait. Surely some of the cars from the service would pass here soon. It wasn't long before several cars drove past, more than she had noticed on the roadside. Perhaps parking had been allowed in a meadow nearby. Her mother would have turned the other way, unless there had been a wake organised somewhere.

After about ten minutes, Gilly decided to return to the church. As she suspected, the lane was now empty, so she pulled up opposite the church gate. Gilly locked her car and made her way into the churchyard. Just ahead of her on the left-hand side, two men were back-filling the grave.

When she reached them, she stopped and asked, "Please could you tell me who has passed away?"

"The Reverend Jacobs, Miss," said one of the men.

"Good heavens. I didn't realise he had died," replied Gilly.

"It was sudden. A massive heart attack, we were told," answered the man.

"That's very sad news. He will be greatly missed."

Gilly walked on, passing the church. She could see a wooden bench with a large yew tree behind it. When she reached the bench, she sat down, wondering why her mother hadn't told her. If she had, Gilly may have attended herself, but then she had only met him recently.

The men were working fast, filling and compacting the soil in the grave. The light was disappearing. Just then, Gilly noticed something strange. She was facing the church tower at the back of the churchyard. What caught her eye was a mist, just above the ground next to the tower, but nowhere else. Her eyes focused on the mist patch for some while, until a loud screech behind her announced a pheasant launching himself into the air.

Distracted, she looked back at the base of the church tower, but the mist had gone. The air seemed much cooler. Reasoning that the cool air had dispersed the mist, she made her way back to her car, saying goodbye to the men before she left.

Chapter 22

Julia needed to talk to her daughter. She needed to tell her about Linden Jacobs. Firstly, that he had died, and then secondly to reveal the information he had passed on. She was not sure how to approach this, and how much she should reveal, and the more she thought about it, the more reluctant she became.

How would Gilly take the news that her father was involved? Perhaps she should let him tell her – after all, he was responsible. But she was sure he would he use his recently diagnosed illness as an excuse, and claim to be unable to remember.

Julia decided to go and see him. She would persuade him to reveal everything he and his friends had done to the Conways. She knew there were other things relating to his past that he wouldn't want his daughter to know. Julia realised she could use the threat of exposing those to make sure he explained. She would be there to make sure Gilly received the whole story.

Julia planned to phone her husband later in the day and arrange a visit, when they could all meet and listen to what he had to say.

Before Julia could call Charles, she received a call from

Gilly asking after Linden Jacobs. Julia apologised that she hadn't told her daughter, explaining that the Reverend had made a list of people who could attend his funeral – mostly people he had known for a long while. He had wanted no fuss, and asked for the ceremony to be as brief as possible.

Once they had spoken, Julia rang Charles. She was very firm, and arranged a visit on Saturday afternoon. He had a habit of not committing, but he knew from her tone she had something on her mind.

Julia arrived at her husband's home as arranged that Saturday afternoon, so she was surprised to find that Charles wasn't ready. He hadn't shaved, his shirt was undone, and his hair was untidy.

"Have I arrived too early for you, dear?" Julia asked.

"Oh, maybe. I'm not sure what time we agreed on. Simple things like this, I'm hopeless with now," replied Charles.

Julia sat down opposite her husband. She told him she had spoken to Linden Jacobs before he died, and mentioned the information he had revealed without going into detail. She expected her husband to become agitated, but he remained calm, slumped in his armchair. For a while there was silence. Julia expected him to say he couldn't recall those events, and waited for him to concoct some sort of excuse.

Charles gave a sigh. "Very well, I'll tell Gilly what happened," he said.

Julia couldn't believe how easily he had agreed, and pressed him to reveal everything, saying she would come with Gilly to give her support.

"Yes, yes, whatever," Charles replied.

Charles arranged for some tea. He seemed mellow and easy-going, a different person from the man she knew. She stayed and talked for a while, not about the Conways, but generally about how he was coping. He seemed very pleasant, unlike the hard-nosed solicitor she knew. Julia left, saying she would ask her daughter to visit the following weekend, if she was available. He seemed happy to oblige.

When Gilly called in to see her mother on Sunday morning, she knew she would be asked to stay for lunch. What she didn't expect was for Julia to ask her to make some time for them both to visit her father the next weekend. Gilly usually called in to see him on Wednesday or Thursday evenings, so she agreed to postpone her visit until the weekend. She asked why, but Julia would only tell her it was very important, and that she must stay calm.

Gilly tried hard to press her mother to give some clue as to why they should meet, but Julia thought it better not to give any information away. A time was arranged for the Saturday afternoon. Gilly would call to see her mother in the morning and, after an early lunch, Julia would drive her over.

Saturday was warm and sunny for the time of year, and

the pair arrived early that afternoon. Charles looked very different today. He had shaved, and was well dressed. Julia wondered what sort of story he would tell, and what would Gilly's reaction be. They sat and discussed his health, the weather, and how the new school was progressing, with Julia wondering when he would talk about his version of events.

Julia gave Charles one of her looks. It was time for their daughter to find out about what had happened all those years ago.

Charles started by apologising that he had caused his daughter to be distressed over the last year, before moving on to give his account of the Conways. The way Charles relayed the story made it sound as if he and his associates were the victims, and the Conways were the villains. Other than that, his version matched Linden's account, and Julia didn't need to add anything at all.

Gilly had for some time suspected that her father had been involved in whatever had happened all those years ago at Underwood House. She knew about his friends, and how greedy they were.

"What happened to the Conways?" she asked. Gilly had heard enough about what awful people they were, and the demands they were making on himself and his poor colleagues.

Charles looked out of the window. He knew his daughter would have no sympathy for him.

"Well, the Conways had to disappear, and disappear for good," was his reply.

"I can hardly believe what I'm hearing. I take it when you say 'disappear,' that they were killed?" Gilly's tone was harsh. She was very angry at what she was hearing. She turned to her mother.

"Did you know about this, Mummy?" she asked, looking directly at Julia.

"Only recently, before Reverend Jacobs passed away," Julia answered.

"How did it happen?" Gilly barked out, looking at her father.

He knew this would not be easy to explain.

"Well, between the four of us we knew some very undesirable characters, and for a large sum of money two of them were happy to oblige," Charles answered in a very shaky voice.

"As easy as that, then? How convenient for you all. Where are these characters now? Who are they?' demanded Gilly.

"I understand they went overseas shortly afterwards," replied Charles.

"Who took care of the bodies?" Gilly was determined to find out all she could.

"Reverend Jacobs arranged for their disposal. I'm

afraid he didn't reveal any details," answered Charles.

"So, he was involved as well? I find that very hard to believe." Gilly's tone grew even harsher.

"He was blackmailed into helping, wasn't he, Charles?" Julia wasn't going to let her daughter think her friend would carry this out without being pressurised.

Charles just nodded as he looked down, avoiding eye contact with them both.

"Where did he bury their bodies, Charles? I imagine that's how he disposed of them," asked Julia. Charles gave his wife a vague look.

"I know where they are buried," said Gilly, realising what she had seen after the funeral.

Both Charles and Julia looked at their daughter.

"How do you know?" asked her mother.

"I think I received another sign. I know exactly where they are."

Both her parents knew better than to doubt her.

"What of Simon?" demanded Gilly.

"Simon lived with Linden and Helen Jacobs," Charles replied. "He was never told what happened, but somehow, he knew. He enjoyed life with them. We funded his education and placed him in a local architect's practice. He made friends easily. Some became rock climbers and encouraged Simon to join them, and it was something he enjoyed immensely. His life was cut short unfortunately while on a climb in Derbyshire. It was a tragic loss for the Jacobs, and in fact for all who knew him,"

"Well, I suppose it's something that he was spared from murder." Gilly felt immensely angry. All she wanted was justice for the Conways. "And now I know what happened, and who is responsible, and where the bodies are buried. Perhaps the police will find these revelations of some interest – assuming the force is no longer corrupted by you and your friends."

Charles shook his head.

"They won't be interested now. And besides, what evidence is there after all this time? I can't go to prison – they'll send me to a hospital to be cared for as I am here. As for my colleagues – one is dead, and the others are in such poor health, exposing us would be pointless."

Gilly felt so angry about what she was hearing. Of course her father was right. There was no proof – she would only have her word, with nothing to support her story.

Charles knew his daughter was beside herself with rage. He knew she would never forgive him, but he was desperate for Gilly and Julia to continue to visit. For the first time in his life, he felt afraid – afraid they would stay away, perhaps returning when he couldn't recognise them.

"Ever since my accident, I have suffered," he said.

There was no response, and no sympathy.

Charles continued. "That year I went skiing alone,

when both of you couldn't come along. You must remember."

Gilly looked at her mother, realising that he was talking about the year of his accident. Julia nodded, wondering what relevance this would have, or what difference it would make.

"I skied with my good friend Ingema. He was a former downhill champion skier. We intended to tackle a slope few others would dare. Ingema had skied it once in his racing days. I managed to persuade him to take me with him so we could come down together. The weather wasn't good at such heights, and the visibility was poor. We made our way high up on the mountain. A breeze picked up and conditions improved slightly, but there was no one else around. Ingema and I put our skies on. He was looking concerned as we stood at the top of the slope, shaking his head.

"'It's too icy,' he explained. 'The speeds will be too excessive. This is not for us today.' Both of us were bitterly disappointed. 'We have to go back,' he said.

"Before we did, he walked away, once he had removed his skis, to relieve himself. As I stood looking down the slope, feeling utterly disappointed, but knowing his judgement was absolutely right, I had the strangest feeling – something I couldn't explain. I turned my head to where Ingema was standing, and I realised someone else was there, right beside me.

"Simon. Simon Newton, who I knew to be dead."

Charles paused, and a look of pain crossed his face.

"He stood there, large as life. I panicked. I was still wearing my skis. I started to slide.

"Ingema was shouting. I was gaining speed, going too fast. I had no control. Stopping was impossible. All I could do was continue. It was terrifying, but I was managing not to fall. Then everything happened so fast.

"I took a corner. Immediately in front was a fallen tree, and that was the last thing I remember.

"The next thing I remember was waking up in hospital. 'You are very fortunate to survive,' the doctor told me. 'A mountain rescue team was training in the area. They were able to reach you quickly.'

"I could feel nothing. No pain. No sensations at all. I could hardly manage to speak. 'Will I recover?' I asked the doctor. He shook his head.

"'You will need to use a wheelchair. That's all I know for now. We shall work on your upper body, but this will take time.' That was all he said, and he was right. It was a long and painful road to recovery."

Charles was looking down at his legs, knowing he would never use them again.

"What a good story," said Julia, sarcastically. "That was quick thinking, Charles, coming up with a punishment for yourself."

Charles shook his head. "I've never revealed any of this until now. I've had to accept my injuries. I suppose I do see them as retribution for my sins."

"I believe him." Gilly was less harsh with her reply, thinking about her own encounter with Simon. "But this doesn't make things right. Is there anything else we should know about these poor, unfortunate people?"

Charles took a few moments to think about whether to add anything to his account.

"Well," he said eventually. "If Simon had lived, he would have become a father."

Both Gilly and Julia looked stunned.

"Simon was very close to a lady in the practice, but she was married. Her husband was more keen on men, and showed very little affection for his wife."

Charles felt he had said enough.

"Who was the lady, then?" asked Gilly.

"Oh, I can't remember now," said Charles, dismissively. "Perhaps the name will come back to me in a day or two."

Julia stood up.

"Continue, Charles, or this will be the last you will see of us."

His wife walked towards the door.

"She was Fiona Harrison," said Charles hastily. "A real beauty, both in looks and nature." Julia returned slowly to her seat.

"Did Simon know about the pregnancy?" asked Gilly.

Charles shook his head. "It was during the very early stages when he died."

"How can you be sure the child was Simon's, then?" Gilly asked.

"As she grew up, there was such a likeness to Simon," said Charles, quietly. "And anyway, Fiona's husband Nigel was infertile. They had tried for a baby in the early years of their marriage with no success."

"So, did this man accept his wife having someone else's child?" Gilly seemed puzzled. "I find that hard to believe."

"I understand he was pleased. They both were. Finally, they had the child they'd wanted. She was the reason they stayed together."

"Are they still around? Locally, I mean. And what was the daughter's name?" Julia was determined to find out all she could while they had the upper hand.

"No, they moved away. I believe Nigel changed jobs. This made things easier, as people round here were making comparisons about their daughter and Simon. Her name was Esther. Esther Harrison."

By now Charles was looking tired and frail. He had said more than he intended, but at last they knew everything. Well – everything he felt he could tell them.

"How did Fiona respond when Simon died?" asked Gilly.

"Oh, it really affected her. I heard she wasn't the same person anymore. However, after Esther was born, she gradually returned to the lovely lady she had been before. That's really all I know."

Charles would say no more.

Gilly and her mother felt it was time to leave. Standing up, moving towards the door, there was only a "Goodbye" and a "Goodbye, Daddy". No hugs or kisses now.

"Please visit again soon. You are welcome anytime," pleaded Charles.

"We'll give this some thought," answered Julia as she opened the door. The pair left without looking back, heading for the car park.

Chapter 23

Neither spoke on the journey home. Gilly had suspected her father would be involved, but not like this. How could he have allowed such things to happen? At home, nothing much more was mentioned until after they had eaten. It was early evening when they sat down together to discuss Charles, and talk about how they would respond to everything he had told them.

It was Julia who made the first move. "He fears we'll disown him."

"What he's done is unforgivable. I know that, and I'm glad he's finally afraid of something," Gilly replied.

"Simon destroyed his life by appearing as he did – if you believe that story," Julia said. "Taking away his freedom so he's had to rely on other people."

"And now he has dementia as well." Gilly shook her head. "This isn't going to be pleasant for anyone."

Julia would not abandon her husband when she knew what she was set to inherit. "I'll visit more often while he still knows who we are," she said.

"I'm not sure I have any pity for him. He deserves everything he gets," said Gilly.

"Perhaps. However, he will always be your father, and he wasn't alone in deciding how to deal with the Conways." Julia was trying her best to stop her daughter from abandoning her father.

"What really frightens me is this daughter, Esther. Esther Harrison," Gilly explained.

"Why are you so concerned about her?" Her mother looked puzzled.

"I feel … I *know* she will return to the area. She'll want to know about her father and his family. She'll ask questions, and Daddy might not be here by then, so the locals who know won't be afraid of him anymore. Everyone will know. This will ruin us all!"

Julia knew that Gilly could not be convinced to believe otherwise. Maybe her daughter was right.

"If, as you say, Esther returns to the area, we shall make out that we're ignorant, and that we know nothing about this at all. I think that would be the best approach. And besides, it may well be many years until she comes back – if indeed she does."

"You've always turned a blind eye, haven't you, Mummy? You've let life go by, accepting things rather than being challenging."

For once, Gilly was opposing her mother. She could see how easy it would be to put the recent revelations to the back of her mind and let life continue as before, but she couldn't let that happen.

"Darling, we can't change what's been done. I can't

accept what has happened any more than you can. If and when Esther appears, we'll meet her. We shall tell her exactly what has happened. To avoid a scandal, and if she is agreeable, we'll offer her compensation."

"Oh, so we buy her off when all she wants is justice? Really, Mummy?" was her daughter's reply.

"In a very short space of time we've learned of this lady's existence, and in your mind her character is very much like your own," Julia commented. "Maybe she'll want justice for the Conway family, and when she learns about your father and his colleagues, with their lives ended or changed forever – maybe this will be enough to satisfy her."

Gilly knew she needed to think things through. Her mother was usually right. She saw things differently, but she had changed her mother's mind. Yes, they would meet Esther, and reveal what they had recently learned.

It was a long evening, filled with much discussion on how their future relations with Charles would be affected by today's revelations. However, they both agreed it would be in all their best interests to remain on good terms, given his deteriorating health.

Although Julia didn't reveal everything her husband had been involved with, she did give a vague hint that he was involved with the building of the new school. He had known that Gilly would be its new headmistress. She also revealed that the reason Jimmy Shaw's construction company had grown so much recently was due to her father's investment in the business.

The next morning, after a late breakfast, Gilly headed home. She knew she needed to pick her life up and try to carry on with some sort of normality, at least until Esther returned. She would devote her life to her work at the school, and she was determined to make sure the move to the new school was a success for children and staff alike.

As for her personal life, that was less clear. Maybe she would get together with Jimmy Shaw. But both of them were always so busy, and they would have to make big changes to their lives … it didn't seem likely.

And there was Esther to consider. Gilly was certain she would appear. Until then, she would plan for that day and decide how best to approach her.

Chapter 24

Gilly's tooth had been causing problems for some while – one of her upper back teeth. She didn't enjoy the dentist, and she had put up with the discomfort for weeks before eventually making an appointment to see Mr Grey. He seemed very pleasant, and let her know that the tooth had split. She would need to make another appointment to have it removed.

This filled Gilly with dread. The dentist was in Aldridge, and she drove to her next appointment hoping for a road closure, or for her car to develop a fault – anything to avoid seeing Mr Grey again.

Gilly had booked an early appointment so she could, if possible, return to school. It was a busy time, just before Easter, and the weather was very good. She parked in the dentist's small car park and made her way to the reception. After seeing the receptionist, she sat in the waiting area and picked up a home and garden design magazine and flicked through the pages.

Two more patients came in and sat down, but Gilly was engrossed in the magazine. She had found a feature about a lady who had renovated a cottage in the North of England. The lady in the photos looked familiar.

She looked younger than Gilly, with a full, curvaceous figure and a perfect peachy complexion. Her hair was blonde to light brown, and cut in a bob, and her features looked soft and lovely.

How did Gilly recognise her? As she read through the article, she realised why. The lady's name was Esther. No mention of a surname.

This was Esther Harrison. Gilly was certain. As she turned the page, behind Esther in another room was a cabinet, and – oh, Lord! – there stood a doll.

Not just any doll.

Bedina, looking straight at her.

"Miss Raymond!"

The dental nurse called for her. With shaking hands, Gilly placed the open magazine on the table. She would have to ask whether it would be alright to take it home when she left.

After an hour, the ordeal was over. The tooth had been difficult to remove and required additional anaesthetic, so Gilly wasn't feeling great. Walking back through the waiting area, she shuffled through the magazines on the table, but there was no sign of the one she had been reading. Only one other lady was waiting, and she wasn't reading anything. Gilly booked a follow-up appointment for after Easter and mentioned the magazine. She was told that people do take them, but sometimes they are returned. If that happened, the receptionist promised to keep it for her.

Gilly decided to go straight home. She could cope with the pain and discomfort, but finding Esther, and knowing she was in possession of Bedina, troubled her severely.

Gilly was desperate to contact Esther to find out how she had obtained Bedina – and to warn her about the doll. After all, her previous owners were no longer alive.

The weather wasn't good over the Easter break, and Gilly didn't venture far at all. She phoned her mother, but made no mention of the magazine, or the article about Esther. As for Jimmy, he seemed to be working more than ever.

The follow-up dental appointment came round. The discomfort had faded, but Gilly knew the dentist was keen to fit her with a denture – something she would resist at all costs. She booked her appointment early, and on the same day as before, hoping to see the same receptionist. She announced her arrival. The receptionist remembered her asking for the magazine, which had been found. This pleased Gilly, and she asked if she could take it with her when she left.

As Gilly had feared, Mr Grey was keen for her to have a tooth replacement. However, Gilly was adamant this wouldn't happen. There had been no problems after the extraction, so the dentist reluctantly agreed. Gilly left for school, collecting the magazine and thanking the receptionist warmly.

That evening, Gilly wrote a letter to the editor of the magazine, asking her to pass on Gilly's details to Esther, hoping she would be in touch. She knew it was a long shot, but she had a feeling that Esther would respond.

A few weeks passed, and Gilly realised that perhaps Esther wasn't interested. She wrote again to the editor, asking her to pass a letter to Esther, in which Gilly had revealed Bedina's troubled past. After all, she needed to know. She received a response from the editor, confirming that her letter had been passed to Esther, and that it would be up to Esther whether to respond, or not. Gilly had read the feature in the magazine many times over. She had an impression of Esther being a lovely, kind lady, someone who cared and was gentle. She realised that revealing Bedina's past would need a very careful approach.

Gilly did hear from Esther, but the letter she received certainly wasn't what she was expecting. It was formal and abrupt. Esther told Gilly they would meet. She gave her a date and a time – neither would be a problem for Gilly – but the location? Underwood House! It was as if Esther already knew. The tone of the letter suggested it would be pointless to try and change anything. If she wanted to meet, she would have to go along with Esther's wishes, and go alone – another of Esther's demands.

Gilly felt nervous about meeting Esther, not to mention meeting at Underwood House.

Chapter 25

The day came. It was spring, and a calm, partly cloudy, partly sunny day. Gilly drove slowly through the village of Westbrook, which looked picture-perfect, and reached the lane that would take her to Underwood House. As she approached the house, she could see a black Range Rover parked in front. The front door was wide open.

She parked, and very nervously walked to the door. As she approached, Esther appeared, just as beautiful as she had seemed in the magazine.

"Good afternoon, Esther." Gilly held out her hand to greet her. "Have you had a pleasant journey?"

Esther made no attempt to shake hands.

"Not your concern," she snapped. "Come inside."

Gilly followed Esther into the kitchen.

"Sit down," Esther commanded.

The pair sat opposite each other at the kitchen table.

"I know everything," Esther began. "I know my father was Simon, and how he went to live with the Conways. I know how the Conways were murdered by your father and his associate, Geoffry Payne."

Esther spoke defiantly. Gilly protested at her calling her father a murderer. Esther looked sterner than ever.

"What would you call it?" She didn't wait for a response. "The Conways were taken from their beds and strapped to chairs. These chairs." Esther shook the chair beside her.

"My father was with Reverend Jacobs that evening!"

Esther ignored the interruption.

"Then Mike and Daphne were placed opposite Emma, all in her bedroom at the back. If they complained, they were beaten with a stick. Then Emma had a cloth stuffed into her mouth, and a hood placed over her head, tied tightly so she couldn't breathe.

"Her parents watched her suffocate. Her chair fell to the floor, and to make sure she was dead, a hot poker was pulled from the fire and pressed onto her skin. In turn, they all died that way, at the hands of these despicable, sadistic, disgusting bastards."

Gilly was furious. How dare this hard-nosed woman describe her father this way?

"So how do you know these things in such detail?" She responded aggressively, but Esther wasn't distracted by Gilly's outburst.

"All the information has come from Bedina," Esther replied. "She can't talk, but she does communicate, in her way. You knew this when you took her hand and wrote your story."

Gilly was shocked. Esther was right, and the fact that she knew about her story was very unnerving. She hadn't mentioned that in her letter.

"At first, Bedina stayed in my bedroom," Esther continued. "While I slept, I was having dreams – awful dreams. I wrote them down, and gradually her life unfolded. I knew about you long before you made contact."

Gilly's tone softened. "How did Bedina come into your life, Esther? Please tell me."

"I knew the McGregors when I was a teenager," Esther explained. "We lived in Carlisle, and some of my friends were into drugs. One was my best friend, and she was buying drugs from them. She took me to their house many times, and they tried to tempt me to try what my friend was buying. I took small amounts for a while until I saw the effect it had on other people. I stopped before I became addicted.

"The thing is – no one suspected Dr McGregor. People thought he was a good man, but I knew he was only interested in making money for himself. When I heard about the fire, I wasn't surprised. I know it was deliberate, but no one found any evidence to suggest that."

Esther looked as stern as ever as she continued her story. "I drove to the fire scene. It was sealed off, but I saw Bedina among the wreckage. No one had taken her. I looked into her eyes, and there was an instant connection between us. I managed to push through the barriers and take her. You see, Gilly, she gets into your mind. She controls and consumes you. She is forever there, inside your head."

Once again Gilly was shocked to hear her suspicions about the McGregors confirmed, but she didn't dare speak up for them.

With that, Esther stood up.

"I'd like to see where the Conways are buried," she demanded.

"You'll need to follow me," Gilly replied.

Gilly stood up, heading for the front door and her car. She waited to see Esther lock the door, and only started her car when she heard the roar of Esther's Range Rover. They soon covered the short distance to the church, and Esther followed Gilly to the side of the tower. Gilly looked down to where she had seen the mist at the side of the tower, while Esther stood beside her.

Without speaking, Esther walked back to her Range Rover, and Gilly followed. Before she got in, Gilly asked, "Is that it? Are you going home?"

"Yes," was Esther's only reply, and with a loud roar and a large cloud of dust she disappeared into the distance.

Gilly stood and watched the dust clear over the empty road.

She had hoped that this disturbing afternoon would bring some closure, but now she wasn't sure. This meeting was never going to be easy – she knew that – but for Esther to be so rude and abrupt was outrageous.

Did Gilly regret making contact? She realised that she did.

Did she regret finding the doll's hand? Yes – certainly.

Gilly wondered why Esther had come all this way to be so insulting. Perhaps she had other business in the area. Maybe she had collected the keys to Underwood House with the intention of buying and renovating it. Maybe Bedina wanted her to live there.

Gilly shook her head. Ever since she had found the doll's hand, her life had been unpredictable. Meeting Simon at the pub, getting to know the McGregors, hearing about the fire, her reaction to Underwood House, the mist in the churchyard – even the strange feeling she'd had at Lola's grave. And finding out about her father's involvement in the Conways' murders – she couldn't guess how this might affect her life in the future.

As she walked to her car, she realised that her life would remain uncertain. She hadn't found certainty in locating Bedina, or meeting Esther, as she'd hoped.

But she found herself smiling. It had been so long since she had discovered the hand, she realised the uncertainty was something she was used to.

After all, she had given Esther the information she needed. Perhaps the doll's story would continue with her new owner. Perhaps Gilly's role in the events of the past was complete.

As she started her car and drove away from Westbrook, she wondered whether she had finally escaped Bedina's influence after all.

Acknowledgements

I would like to thank Nathan and all staff at Softwood Books for contributing to my novel.

Many thanks to Penny and Lesley, my first readers, for writing such great reviews.

A big thank you to my partner, Elizabeth, for all her support.

Author Bio

Through his work in garden construction, Richard met many interesting characters and was told stories that revealed intriguing connections between people. These encounters prompted ideas and inspired him to write *The Doll's Hand.*